DEREK MAUL

Derek Maul

ALSO BY DEREK MAUL

Get Real: A Spiritual Journey for Men

In My Heart I Carry a Star: Stories for Advent

The Unmaking of a Part-Time Christian

Reaching Toward Easter

10 Life-Charged Words: Real Faith for Men

Pilgrim in Progress: Notes from the Journey

In God's Image

SUDDENLY THE LIGHT WAS GONE

A novel of World War Two

Derek Maul

DRM
BOOKS

Derek Maul

SUDDENLY THE LIGHT WAS GONE:
A Novel of World War Two

Website: derekmaul.com
Blog: derekmaul.blog

Cover image: Ely Cathedral; Andrew Sharpe, SharpeImages.co.uk

Maul, Derek, 1956 –
Suddenly the Light was Gone/Derek Maul
ISBN-978-1544128894
ISBN-1544128894

Novel/Historical Fiction
Young Adult

Derek Maul

"For behold, the darkness shall cover the earth,
And deep darkness the people;
But the LORD *will arise over you,*
And His glory will be seen upon you."
(Isaiah 60:2)

Derek Maul

Derek Maul

Dedication

To my amazing daughter, Naomi, who has championed this book since the very beginning. Without her persistence, enthusiasm, encouragement, and belief this manuscript would not exist. To my remarkable son, Andrew, who continues to teach me what it means to be a citizen of the world. To their spouses, Craig and Alicia, who have expanded my joy. To my grandchildren, David and Beks, who are already captivated by reading. And – always - to my gifted and wise wife, Rebekah, who constantly translates belief into light, love, grace, and blessings. This book belongs to you all.

Contents

Introduction

Henry's Story:

Derek Maul

INTRODUCTION
ENGLAND
- MAY 1990

Henry Bradley climbed out of the taxicab, carefully crossed Sandgate Road, and then walked the hundred yards or so to the seaside town's signature clifftop gardens. He paused in front of the William Harvey monument, noted the spatter of fresh seagull droppings that garnished the famous physician's bronze likeness, shook his head, and smiled. After a moment or two he turned and made his way to the overlook.

There, looking out across Folkestone's seafront to the English Channel and the continent of Europe beyond, Henry closed his eyes, drinking deeply of the fresh salt air. He shivered a little in the fifty-five degree breeze, and tried to recall the way it all looked when he had last stood in that very spot, more than a lifetime ago.

It was exactly forty-five years since Henry had left the town, taking in one final view of the harbor, the beaches, and the white cliffs of nearby Dover - and an even fifty since the memorable day he'd stood on the hills behind the town with his best friends, hurling insults at Hitler and thumbing their noses at the menacing German army, vowing to defend England's green and pleasant lands with everything they had.

Those days felt like another age in history, almost a story he had read about in a book, an adventure that had happened to someone else. Henry sighed, thrust his hands into the pockets of his windbreaker, turned to his right, and started to walk through the manicured park that ran along the top of the bluffs for the best part of a mile, making his way toward the place where the old bandstand had stood during his childhood.

I'll be in trouble if it's not there anymore, Henry thought to himself. *Who crosses the Atlantic Ocean to meet someone in a place that may not even exist? Well, it's too late to make any other plans now...*

*　　　　*　　　　*　　　　*

"Henry Bradley?"

The greeting came from a woman sitting at the top of the bandstand steps. One hand shielded her eyes from the glare; the other cradled a serious looking camera. She wore stylish jeans, a long leather jacket, and expensive walking shoes. Her dark brown hair was tucked under a man's tweed hat.

"Who wants to know?" Henry couldn't help but smile as she stood up to greet him.

"Elizabeth Crenshaw," she smiled in return, "on assignment for *History Profiles Magazine*." Her eyes sparkled in a way that spoke of life and intelligence.

"But wait a minute," Henry said. "You don't sound British."

"Ironically, I'm the exact opposite of you," Elizabeth laughed. "I was born in the United States, attended college in Florida, did an internship in London, then ended up settling in Canterbury, right here in Kent."

"But - unlike me - you're a very long way from being retired," Henry said, discreetly calculating her age and coming up with a number somewhere approximating the low to mid-forties.

"Very gracious of you, I'm sure. But I'm closer than you think; I turn fifty-five next month."

Henry couldn't believe it. But he also understood all too well the effect attitude, passion, and health have on aging. Other than a couple of letters and one phone conversation, this was the first time he'd actually met the reporter who seemed so genuinely interested to hear his story. It was obvious Elizabeth Crenshaw had a youthful spirit and a pile of energy.

"Coffee, or lunch?" she said. "I've been told to spare no expense on per diem, so long as it's somewhere south of ten pounds a day!"

"Well in that case lead me to the very best coffee bar you know," Henry said. "And if it involves some vague approximation of a warm Danish pastry, then I promise I'll spring for seconds myself."

"Walk this way," Elizabeth said, offering her arm, "I know just the place."

*　　　　　*　　　　　*　　　　　*

Ten minutes later Henry found himself sitting in a deep, expansive leather chair in a quiet corner of what was once the lobby of a dignified hotel. He had a tall mug of coffee in one hand – ceramic, not Styrofoam, the last bite of a chocolate Danish in the other, and the full attention of an unnervingly captivating magazine writer.

"My first question is seriously important," Elizabeth said. "I honestly can't begin to write any kind of story until I make sense of this. It's been bothering me ever since you said you would do the interview in person."

"Fire away." Henry took another sip of his coffee.

"Why not just talk to me on the phone?" she said. "Taking a trip like this has to be a major inconvenience, to say nothing of the expense."

Henry smiled and shook his head. "You're not the only one who noticed it's the 50th anniversary of Dunkirk."

He held his hands out in a gesture that suggested he'd thought a lot about this over the past few days.

"On this very day a half century ago I stood on the hills behind this town with my best friends. We were defiant, and we dared Hitler to take another step closer. Of course we had no idea of the extent of what was beginning to unfold, just a few miles to the east in Belgium.

"But we knew soon enough!" Henry smiled sheepishly. "So I guess I have simply come to the realization it's well past time I took a long trip down memory lane…."

For a moment, emotion threatened to interrupt his thoughts. There was so much to tell, and he really didn't know where to start. Elizabeth waited.

"Back in 1948 I took a steamer to America for a one-year stint as an attaché at the British embassy. One year! Good grief! I had no idea how quickly the world would shift, how my life would change, or that it would be this long before I got back to Folkestone. It seemed like a coincidence my retirement worked out this close to the anniversary. But the more I thought about it, the more everything felt like the hand of providence."

Providence? Henry thought to himself. *Where did that idea come from?*

"You're saying it's like you felt compelled to come?" The reporter leaned forward in her chair.

"I don't exactly know. You put together the puzzle pieces," Henry said quietly, shrugging his shoulders, hands turned upwards in a gesture of irresolution. "I've been thinking about retirement for a couple of years. I wanted to do something big to launch this new time in my life. Then Deborah passed away just before Christmas…"

Elizabeth gasped. "Your wife? Oh my goodness, I'm so sorry. I had no idea…"

"How could you have known?" Henry shrugged again. "These things happen. I only mention it because her passing is a huge part of the reason I decided to take this trip…

"Fact is, I've been thinking about my old home quite a lot over the past few months," he said as he sipped some more coffee. "Then your letter came, asking me to comment about this very significant anniversary of the evacuation at Dunkirk. And that caused me to think about so much more…."

Henry paused again, as if he was calibrating exactly what he should say before he continued.

"And suddenly everything became crystal clear," he said.

"And what do you mean by that?" Elizabeth interjected.

Henry smiled. "I knew it was time to put some fresh flowers on my father's grave."

For a moment, or maybe two, the silence hung in the air like a heavy mist. Before even those few seconds had passed, Elizabeth intuitively understood that this was less a straightforward writing assignment, and more a journey into the soul of the man sitting across from her.

"I don't mean to be obtuse, or mysterious," Henry said, watching the reporter's expression shift from simple curiosity to something more. "But I'm honestly still trying to process everything for myself. How about I just answer your questions, one at a time, and we can see where the conversation goes from there?"

"Fair enough," Elizabeth replied. "So let's start exactly right where we were - with your dad – if that's okay?"

He nodded.

"You mentioned it was time for some fresh flowers. So when exactly did your father pass away? How old were you? And how long has it been since there were any fresh flowers that you know of?"

Henry stood up, walked to the window, and stared out toward the seafront.

"Let me grab a refill," he said. "You?"

"I'm fine, thanks," she replied. Elizabeth remained patient, biding her time, reserved. She had learned enough about interviews over her long career to understand that listening was far more important than writing.

A minute or two later Henry was back in the deep leather chair; poised, alert, ready, as if he had come to a decision about which door to open first.

"You got out of the blocks with a seriously big first question." Henry looked at his watch and raised one eyebrow, a faint smile forming at the edges of his mouth. "So how long have you got?"

Elizabeth leaned forward in her seat expectantly. "I guess I can pitch a different question if that's what you want," she said, pretty sure he'd field it anyway.

"No, no, it's okay," Henry responded. "I guess I did kind of leave the invitation open, didn't I? Besides, I'm fairly sure we'd end up having to get back to the topic eventually."

"Is that because your father's death is important to our story about the anniversary of Dunkirk?" Elizabeth queried. "Or because it reveals another reason you flew back home?"

"Because it's that important to me!" Henry said, strongly. "On some level it's the whole entire story. Listen - if my story fits snugly with what your magazine is looking for, then fine. If not, then fine too."

Elizabeth flinched. Henry was surprised at himself, his own reaction, and how sensitive he had sounded.

There was another pause, a long one. This time the silence was even more loaded. Elizabeth realized she'd driven down from Canterbury to meet with a man she didn't know even a little bit. The story was intriguing, yes, but Henry Bradley was obviously complicated. What if he couldn't handle the interview? What if he was going to be difficult? What if she was wasting her time?

Henry sensed her disquiet.

"I'm sorry," he said. "Forgive me. I guess I'm more sensitive about this than I realized. I'm jetlagged, out of balance, and emotional on top of it all. But the connection between my father's death and this fiftieth anniversary of the Dunkirk evacuation is… how can I say it… everything.

"Then, and this is just as true, May 1940 – exactly fifty years ago - is to some extent simply a marker, a punctuation-point in time that's helping me remember. This anniversary is something that has given me just the excuse I needed, the impetus to cross the Atlantic yesterday. It's okay, really, I get it. I understand that you have to ask hard questions as to how it all fits together."

"But then at some point, eventually, I have to understand too," Elizabeth said, cautiously, "or I won't be in any position to explain any of it to my readers."

Henry nodded - more to himself than the reporter – trying to figure out just how complex and how deep this conversation was going to be. *A little more than that sixty-minute Q & A you were looking for, huh?* As if he was wondering how far down this rabbit hole he should go. As if he was in effect giving himself permission to continue.

"The short answer to the question," he said, "goes like this. Dad died in 1940. It was late July; he was forty-eight years old."

"Good grief," Elizabeth found herself surprised at the timing of a death for the second time in just a few short minutes. "That has to be right at the beginning of the story. Do you have any brothers or sisters?"

"No. My parents were both in their thirties when they married, and apparently I made a rather dramatic entry into this world," Henry said. "Long story short, another child was never a safe option."

"And your mother?"

"Lung cancer, 1952."

"I'm sorry, Henry. So what exactly happened with your dad in the summer of 1940?"

"Ironically, it was a freak accident," Henry said. "He turned out to be one of the few casualties of the war the Germans honestly didn't intend to target!

"A damaged German bomber was limping away from some raid gone wrong, and the pilot ended up way off course. The plane was on fire and losing altitude rapidly. It looks like the guy tried to land in a field but instead crashed into the train dad was riding. Witnesses say it was obvious the pilot was doing his best to avoid hitting the train, but the leading edge of one wing just clipped the last carriage. Dad's section derailed, rolled off the embankment, and slammed into the bulwark of a bridge."

Henry paused to let the image sink in.

"It happened just a couple of miles west of Newmarket, on the London train."

Elizabeth scribbled furiously on her notepad. "Newmarket? That's where the racetracks are, up near Cambridge, right? But my notes say you grew up here in Folkestone? I think you mentioned somewhere that your dad was a doctor. What was he doing on a train in the middle of East Anglia?"

Henry sipped his coffee, settled deep into his chair, and smiled generously. "Now that's the story, isn't it?

"Remember when I asked you how much time you really have? I wasn't kidding. I can't even begin to explain that part of the story if we don't back up at least a few months. So let's start at the very beginning."

"Why don't you tell me what you mean by 'beginning'," she said. "Then we can take it from there."

Elizabeth was starting to relax again. *This is going to be a lot more than an article,* she thought to herself. *This could be a series, or even an entire book!*

"To find the beginning you could ask me about what I was doing fifty years ago today," Henry said, "or if a kid like me had any clue as to what war really meant? Maybe you could ask me about how well I was getting along with my dad in May of 1940? Or ask something about my best friends, Charlie and Graham?"

Elizabeth could read the intensity in his voice. The emotion was still very much in evidence, just below the surface. She wondered if they should break for a couple of hours - or call it a day. She felt she needed to give Henry some time to find his feet. But at the same time she didn't want to, because by now she was well beyond interested.

"I'll bite," she said. "So tell me, Henry Bradley, what were you doing fifty years ago today? You were just fifteen years old, and the evacuation of Dunkirk was about to get under way. Did you have any idea how serious things were going to get?"

"Not a clue, Elizabeth! I was a teenager, and I thought the world revolved around me," Henry said. "I loved my carefree life with my friends, and I resented the looming intrusion of one day having to grow up."

He shook his head again, slowly. "Boy did that ever change in a hurry!"

Henry took another sip of coffee, scratched the top of his head, and slipped into his best storyteller mode. The words came easily, and the emotions too. He felt, almost, fifteen again.

Before long, "Elizabeth the Reporter" turned into "Elizabeth the Transfixed." She was completely drawn in.

"I'm probably going to sound a lot like a self-absorbed teenager at first," Henry said by way of introduction. "But it's the only voice I have for setting the stage. I may be newly retired, but every time I start to talk about the war my inner teenage boy wants to take over."

Elizabeth settled into a corner of the sofa, made sure her tape recorder was working, added a couple of notes to her yellow legal pad, and got the ball rolling with a couple of questions.

Then, almost like a new guest invited into the conversation, Henry's "inner teenager" scrambled through a fissure in the space-time continuum to share his story. For the next few hours - and with an increasingly confident (and eventually more adult) voice – he began to tell the story of 1940, and how the war changed everything, and everybody, forever.

Derek Maul

Derek Maul

CHAPTER ONE
HENRY'S STORY
- 1940

Trouble at Home and in Europe

My perspective may not always come across sounding fair, or reasonable, but I guess I'm always going to think of 1940 as the year "Dr. Doom" finally came up with a good enough excuse for kicking me out. I was fifteen years old, it seemed like I was constantly at odds with my father's way of looking at the world, and I was convinced he wanted me out - out of the house, and out of his hair.

Sure, there was a war on, I understood that, but to me all the talk about "evacuation" didn't even begin to add up or make sense. Hitler and his Nazis were not about to target our house – out of all the others – just because I stayed home with my family. Of course not.

The real reason, or so I believed, was likely more along the lines of the soccer ball against the side of the house, the cricket ball through the kitchen window, the consistently hit-or-miss chores, the lack of weeding in my father's vegetable garden, the tense pattern of arguments we had fallen into, and the stuff a few of my teachers had been complaining about. Oh, and I guess maybe that incident down by the harbor. To tell the truth, I had never been a deliberate troublemaker, and I genuinely wanted peace with my dad. But – honestly - I could never seem to find the right words to tell him.

Fact is we just didn't get along, and neither one of us seemed motivated to get things set in the right direction. I irritated him, he annoyed me. The status quo was what it was, and we mostly tried to stay out of each other's way. The malfunction was as simple, and as complete, as that.

If my father was the one telling the story, you'd likely hear some theory about a child with behavior problems, a story about loving parents dealing with a troublesome adolescent, shame and disappointment, poor decisions by yours truly, life with their unruly and perplexing teenager, and – apparently more important to my father than anything else - embarrassment for a respected member of the community.

The way I saw it, at least at the time, was that my dad liked to cast himself as, "Mr. Affronted" – principled, misunderstood, wounded, and disrespected.

But here's the thing, I wasn't buying the whole victim scenario. It wasn't just me that was rude, it wasn't just me that started fights, and it wasn't just me that argued. I'd say we both had a problem. I'd say things needed to get better.

To be honest, I knew I was at least somewhat responsible, and it really did bother me when things went wrong between us. If only dad would ease up just a little bit, maybe give an inch or two, if only he'd meet me even part of the way there.

I really wasn't that bad of a kid. But I was beginning to think my dad believed I was a total loss.

Anyway, once the war got going and everyone started to panic like the whole place was going to blow up, I knew right away what was, inevitably, going to happen to me. I was tagged to be ditched, first chance my father got. I could see it clearly, as if a preview of the upcoming play-by-play was nicely displayed in some kind of a crystal ball.

Once hostilities with Germany were officially declared, whole trainloads of kids were being packed up and sent away to what the people in charge called "safety," one school at a time from all over the southeast of England. The government called the initiative, "Operation Pied Piper." I called it a setup, I called it my dad's golden opportunity to get me out of his space.

Kids from the London schools had been sent away first, close to the end of 1939. It was the biggest evacuation in history, and pretty much all the children in the city had been cleared out in just a few days.

Then – and this was a big surprise to everyone - everything turned quiet. The United Kingdom stood on the brink of destruction, facing the greatest threat since the Norman invasion of 1066, but without much noticeable action to speak of. The entire nation held its breath, and the newspapers started calling it, "The Phony War."

Meanwhile, in my hometown, just a few miles from mainland Europe, my friends and I were convinced we knew exactly what was going to happen, and that it was going to happen very soon. We lived in the seaside town of Folkestone - the exact closest point in all of England to continental Europe. We understood that, eventually, our part of the south coast was destined to come into the line of fire.

The reports coming in from Germany were horrifying. But – by the time the stories trickled down to my friends and me - it all had the distant quality of our school history books, of things happening to other people who lived a long way away, and a long time ago.

There was even word that Herr Hitler did not want to think of England as the enemy of Germany. Rumors circulated suggesting that *der Führer* admired the British way of life, and that the German dictator would be happy to leave us all alone, if only England would nod, wink, and give him a free hand to do what he wanted in Europe.

More telling, and more in tune with the way all my friends felt, was the widespread belief that, "it simply would not happen here." It could not happen to us, we reasoned, because things like that only took place in other countries, and involved other people. Nice kids from nice families in a nice country are automatically issued some kind of a free pass, right?

*   *   *   *

Phony War or not, by May 1940 German forces had successfully occupied France and Belgium, one mile at a time and with chilling efficiency. With much of the European continent overrun by Nazis, it was tough to turn a blind eye anymore. Things were looking grim for our proud little island, and with the French seaport of Calais just twenty-two miles away, directly across the English Channel, we didn't have to look far to run into real and present danger.

In consequence, there was barbed wire strung up everywhere, razor sharp and roll upon roll. New gun batteries had started to spring up in strategic locations. Rumor had it the harbor approaches were being mined, and we were told not only to stay off the beaches, but far, far away from anything interesting.

My friends and I were witness to a wide range of mysterious yet purposeful activity. Troop movements were evident in nearly every part of the town, and – especially for the grownups - there was a huge burden of anxiety.

All told, for some curious teenaged boys, this menacing turn of events meant more interesting action in our own backyard than my friends and I could have hoped or dreamed for.

But, somehow, I always seemed to manage to get myself into trouble. Trouble wasn't exactly my strategy of choice, but neither was the tame alternative of keeping my distance as advised. So it pretty much happened that trouble was – for better or for worse - simply how things usually turned out.

C HAPTER TWO

Plotting Against Hitler, and Making Plans for Mischief

My two best friends were Charlie Green and Graham Fern. We'd been in school together since we were five, and we did everything as a team. We were always on the move, riding our bikes absolutely everywhere, all the way from the hills, into town, through the many parks, and down to the seaside. We were fast, we were stealthy, we kept our eyes open, and we knew all the shortcuts.

My street led down to the edge of a public golf course. Our favorite jaunt had us circle through the adjacent playing fields, race down Cherry Garden Lane, then bike on up to Waterworks Hill. That's where we could walk out to our favored lookout on Caesar's Camp, the tallest elevation on our section of the North Downs. Our vantage point commanded a wide view from the White Cliffs of Dover, through the town of Folkestone, and around to the long, curling bay that stretched out beyond Hythe to the Dungeness headland, as well as the boggy marshland between, the historic refuge of famous smugglers like Thorndike's popular literary hero, Dr. Syn.

In the spring of 1940 it was all ours, everything we could see or imagine - or at least as much of it as our friends in the army would allow. And, by and large, the guys in uniform weren't a bad lot. Well, not so long as we stayed out of trouble - which, of course, we did not.

Late one sunny afternoon we sat on the hilltop together, talking about the war as we surveyed our domain. It was Sunday, May 26, 1940. We had our shirtsleeves rolled up, and the soft late spring daylight stretched long into the evening. Graham was flat on his stomach, propped up on his elbows, chewing the fat end of a long piece of sweet grass, shirt tail un-tucked as per usual, half unkempt hair hanging longer than the rest of us could ever seem to get away with.

"In the morning, let's go to the harbor," Graham said. "There's a lot more interesting stuff behind the guard post since the last time we checked."

"We can't just skip school," Charlie observed. Like me, Charlie was attracted to Graham's ideas, and - like me - he was nervous about potential trouble. "Let's wait 'till next Saturday."

"No can do," Graham retorted. "Saturday there will be kids everywhere, and a bunch more people downtown. This way no one will even know we're around. Trust me."

Both of them looked at me, I was always the deciding vote. *Thanks a lot, guys, this way it's my fault whatever we end up doing. Heck,* I thought, *why waste a good opportunity to have some fun?*

"Let's leave home for school at the usual time," I said. "But then we're going to have to take coordinated evasive action. How about we meet behind the bandstand up on top of the cliffs at nine fifteen? Then we'll plan our strategy. Nine-thirty we head down to the docks. If you're late, you're on your own, or I guess you'll have to catch up.

"Agreed?"

"Absolutely."

"You bet."

It sounded like a good plan at the time.

We looked down the hill and over the broad vista of home and safety, familiarity spread out all across the mile or two that lay between our lookout and the waterfront:

- A simple gray rectangle of solid concrete dock neatly finished off the view of the sandy bay.
- The harbor gave shelter to the coastal fishing fleet that had started the town and its original industry hundreds of years before.
- The light blue waters, typically teeming with vessels in peacetime, were quiet.
- In the distance, a distinct white line marked the chalky cliffs of Northern France.

"I listened to the radio after lunch," I said. "You remember the news about how Boulogne fell to the Germans a few days ago?"

My friends nodded. We were all paying more attention to the BBC than we ever had before.

"Well, apparently today they occupied Calais."

It was a clear day, so we could just see a few of the French coastal town's tallest buildings, peeking out over the horizon, highlighted by the late afternoon sun. Divisions of enemy troops, just twenty-five miles away, were gathering to invade England.

"Do you think there were kids on these hills watching out for William the Conqueror back in 1066," Charlie said, "before he came across the channel and kicked King Harold's ass at the Battle of Hastings?"

"He wasn't called William *the Conqueror* until after he landed and won the battle, dumbass," Graham countered. "Until then he was just William."

"Well maybe *der Führer* will be remembered as, Hitler *the Loser*!'" I suggested hopefully.

"You bet," Graham said. "He'd better watch out if he wants to try anything aggressive with the three of us here!"

Charlie shivered, stood up, and made a move for his bike. Graham and I followed. The light was about gone and we had to get home pronto. I hoped my dad was still out, I didn't feel like any kind of an inquisition.

"Nine-fifteen. Be there."

"Right. Cheerio then."

"Cheerio."

CHAPTER THREE

What Could Possibly Go Wrong?

The next morning, riding my bike along Castle Hill Avenue and trying my best to keep a low profile, I found it a challenge not to feel blatantly conspicuous. I felt like a clown in a toy car. "Stealthy" isn't exactly an option when you're in school uniform, it's several minutes after the nine o'clock attendance bell, and you're headed in the exact opposite direction from where you're supposed to be.

My red and black school tie, as always, was doing its best to strangle me. So I twisted and pulled with one hand, finally worked it loose, and stuffed the offending emblem deep into my blazer pocket. I felt a combination of partial relief and guilt.

Occasionally, on a seriously hot summer's day, our headmaster would stand up at morning assembly and make a rare but welcome announcement. "Boys," Mr. Bryan would say in his best, "I'm trying not to sound permanently annoyed but I am, and I simply can't help myself," voice. "Boys... you may loosen your ties a half inch, and unfasten the top button of your shirts."

Typically a murmur of appreciation would buzz around the room, followed by a faint smattering of applause, as if some great act of humanitarianism had been performed. In our school we took the small gifts of charity we were given and enjoyed them, because we never knew when such glad munificence might unexpectedly be visited upon us again.

The ride from my house up to the cliff-top public park has always been one of my favorites. Old cherry trees line the avenue, a generous grass verge has been left between the sidewalk and the street, and well maintained homes make for a picture-postcard setting.

That morning I caught a whiff of the sweet cherry blossom from where much of it lay matted on the side of the road beneath the trees. The fragrant air encouraged my sense of adventure, helping diminish any feelings of remorse in response to riding directly away from my teachers and my morning classes.

After a few minutes I approached the commercial section leading up to Sandgate Road. The trees petered out, some of the shops were already open, and the sidewalks were populated with people obviously caught up in their own concerns. But I still felt the need to move with extreme caution. It would not be easy to dodge – or answer - probing questions about what I was doing, and why I had wandered so far away from school.

I crossed the busy road carefully, trying to keep a low profile. Then, once I reached the other side, I dismounted my bike, walking purposefully along Clifton Gardens until the road dead-ended at the enormous statue of Dr. William Harvey. Often described as "the father of modern medicine," the celebrated doctor looked out with massive dignity, his fixed gaze falling somewhere between the flowers and the gray-blue waters of the English Channel.

I had to laugh. Not only did Harvey inspire the founding of our illustrious school back in 1674, but he was also one of my father's greatest heroes. Dr. William Harvey was the medical pioneer credited with discovering the circulatory system of the blood, somewhere around 1618. His brilliant ideas were initially dismissed as "crack-brained" by most of his colleagues, but he persisted, becoming an icon of scientific rigor and medical investigation. I could imagine Dr. Harvey stalking the cemeteries at night, digging up corpse after corpse, inquisitively slicing grizzly cadavers until he had opened enough veins and arteries to prove his theory.

I'm pretty sure my dad wanted to be a medical genius more than anything else in the world. He was a good doctor, as general practitioners go, and he maintained a respected practice in the center of the town. He was well known and even admired locally, but he would never be famous in the way he wanted. I think he knew it, because his second greatest ambition was for me to be his alter ego and to do it for him.

I wasn't so sure. Work my butt off? Take advanced level science courses? Vie for competitive admission to Oxford or Cambridge? Saturate myself in research, and internships, and residency, and fellowships? Spend more time in libraries and less playing games? See my entire life absorbed in medicine? I don't think so, no thank you very much! It was just another way, I suppose, that I disappointed him, just another way I made him angry.

The huge monument to Harvey certainly looked impressive, but I would have been happier to see a statue of Charles Dickens or maybe George Bernard Shaw, a couple of my favorite "local" writers. Both Dickens and Shaw were frequent sojourners in Folkestone, churning out some fairly radical work while on extended stays. But it was Harvey who made the headlines. He was immortalized through science and celebrated as the founder of our school (celebrated tediously, and at every possible opportunity) for going on three hundred years.

To some of us, however, the great theorist and surgeon was best remembered via the magic of a contraband photograph that circulated the campus for the best part of a week earlier that spring. The shoot had been the brainchild of a group of the "Upper 6th" boys (seniors), and it took the school by storm.

The photo featured three anonymous students who could be observed from the rear – in school uniform – appearing to relieve themselves on the famous statue of the great doctor. Almost every boy in the school had seen the picture. Our headmaster, Mr. Bryan, had responded as expected with a close to full-blown tantrum at a school-wide assembly one morning. He was beyond enraged. Without the cooperation of such a consistently unhinged head of staff, such efforts would always be destined to fall short of immortality. If there was one thing we could always count on, it would be for our notoriously tightly wound leader to blow a gasket pretty much on cue.

Beyond the statue, lush green parkland stretched for more than a mile along the top of the thickly vegetated escarpment that distinguished the Folkestone bluffs from the stark white chalk cliffs of neighboring Dover. Riding my bike past the scores of sculptured flowerbeds and finely manicured lawns, I breathed deeply the natural peace of it all. It seemed impossible that, only a few miles away, Europe was being torn apart by the ravages of a rapidly escalating war.

"So what kept you, Bradley? Slow down to smell the pretty flowers?" Graham Fern was already lounging on a bench behind the bandstand, arms thrown back so he used the entire width of the seat, chewing on his ever present piece of grass.

"Seen Charlie yet?"

"Nope."

"Check it out," Graham said, pulling off his backpack. "How's this for provisions?" Always thinking of food, he threw me the bag for closer inspection.

It was generously stuffed with plentiful rations.

"Pretty damn good," I said. "Did you ask?"

"Did I ask? Right. Why didn't I think of that, what a great idea! And I also told my mum and dad where to find me if they wanted to bring us all some extra grub."

He snapped his tie at me before throwing it in his pack. "Hey, you want to ditch the uniform?"

"I don't think so." Somehow the stories we'd read about spies, captured and shot when they were discovered behind enemy lines in civilian clothing, lingered in my imagination. Didn't they treat prisoners better if you were caught looking more like a regular soldier than an agent of espionage?

I think Graham was having some of the same thoughts, because he kept his jacket on too.

Just as we were about to go on without him, Charlie Green flew round the corner and jumped off his bike with a worried look all over his face.

"Police..." he panted between gasps. "They. Must. Know." Pant... "What. We're." Pant... "Up. To." Pant. Gasp. Pant.

"What do you mean, 'know what we're up to?'" I laughed. "We don't even know what we're up to yet. Where are they, anyway? Did any of them follow you?"

Derek Maul

"Probably," Charlie said. "I saw them back on Sandgate road. Two of them, both on their bikes."

"Did they even see you?" asked Graham.

"Couldn't help it. I knocked the big one right off his bike when I hit his back tire coming up Castle Hill Avenue!"

"You did what?"

"Holy Moly!"

"We're out of here."

"Follow me," Graham said quickly. "Get on your bikes. I know just the place."

Graham jumped on his bike and headed off in the direction of the community concert hall, a massive building set directly into the heart of the steep bluffs. Charlie and I peddled close behind. There was a footpath that started just behind the enormous balcony, and he raced his bike around the first turn before disappearing down the side of the cliff.

Before much more than 30 seconds had passed, we were well on our way down the second section of "The Zig-Zag Path," the steep winding flower and rock garden that meandered its way down to the quieter section of seafront known as Lower Sandgate.

"Quick. Let's hide in here." Graham suddenly cut left and into the rock face.

"This cave will make a great safe house if they think to look this far down..."

"Which I doubt they will," Charlie interrupted, "because I forgot to mention the small traffic accident that got their attention right after I tried to apologize and they quit waving their arms at me. It wasn't serious, but it's going to take everyone a long time to clean up all the sandbags and stuff the army truck was carrying when it hit the bus."

Graham and I took turns smacking him with our caps.

"Okay, I guess that was a good way to start the morning," I laughed. "A little practice won't hurt in case we really do have to run for it."

"You really think there's a possibility we'll get caught?" Charlie asked. He was genuinely concerned about getting into real trouble, and it was written all over his face.

"It wouldn't be any fun if there wasn't at least a small chance of something going wrong!" Graham replied, reasonably. "But, like I said, this is the perfect day for a little creative snooping."

Graham offered his contagious grin as a measure of reassurance. Then he looked around for something fresh to chew on.

CHAPTER FOUR

One Bad Idea after Another

"Here's the plan..." Graham drew us close, as if there might be someone trying to listen in. "Let's ride back through the gardens at the top. Then we can take a good look at everything from up there. The view is perfect. We can tweak the details before we cruise on down to the harbor."

We rode back along the top of the cliffs, nonchalantly. Past the bandstand, past rows and rows of well-manicured flower beds, and past William Harvey, whose dignity was even at that moment being violated by a number of large seagulls. We peddled down to the end, where one of the seaside classic "penny for three minutes" telescopes overlooked the harbor.

We looked long and hard, checking out the security gate, the guards, the docks, the boats, the English Channel, and the ominous Nazi occupied continent of Europe. Then we parked our bikes against the cliff edge railing and leaned over, angling for the best possible look at the seaport below.

"I can never get over how miniature everything seems when we're looking this far down." Charlie stood on the lower rail, his long, skinny body hanging out over the vegetation that held the cliff face together.

"Check out the train coming in, it looks just like a model in a toy store window," Charlie said. "Did you know it's the steepest gradient for a regular track in all England? Look! Fifteen boxcars, loaded, plus a platform that looks like it's carrying some kind of a big gun. They have two locomotives at each end."

I followed his gaze as the train made its way through the inner harbor. "Can you imagine what it would be like to float under the arches in a fishing boat while a train was clattering overhead?"

"Sounds like a plan for the next adventure," Graham said. "But who knows if the people heading out in the boats today are going to catch the fish they're looking for and get home safely, or maybe end up running into some enemy U-boat?"

The harbor area was bustling with activity. Using the telescope, we could see uniformed military personnel just about everywhere. Checkpoints, barriers, guard stations, and fenced-off storage areas were scattered randomly throughout the complex. It looked like the activity of a nation expecting to be invaded at any minute – which, it turns out, was a definite possibility.

We three boys, though, had supreme confidence in the British Expeditionary Forces (BEF), the divisions who were fighting to slow down the German advance in Belgium and the north of France. "Our boys" would win the day, and then this war would be over before it hardly got going. We were confident of it.

What we didn't know or even suspect was exactly what was going on in Belgium that very day (and would be unfolding for the coming week). Unbeknownst to us, the retreating Allied forces had already started to pour onto the beaches at Dunkirk. We had heard reports about the German presence in Calais. The town was literally within eyesight from where we were standing, but we had no idea about the critical, perilous, and growing more desperate by the moment danger England was facing.

Even as we stood on the top of the cliffs, overlooking the harbor and planning our schoolboy shenanigans, the beaches of Belgium were overflowing with tens of thousands of desperate, retreating, stranded, bloodied, battered, defeated British troops.

If this war was going to be over soon, then it wasn't going to be "Our Boys" mopping up Nazis... it was more than likely going to be the other way around.

But, like I said, we didn't know.

"It looks like the barbed wire from the water goes all the way up to the main gate," Graham said, swinging the telescope around. "There's no way in via that route."

"Why is the wire all sitting out in rolls like that?" Charlie wondered out loud. "Couldn't they just string it up like a fence?"

"My cousin fought in The Great War," Graham said. "He told me the wire cutters make it too easy to get through when it's just strung out. When they have rolls and rolls of razor wire like we have here, then it's just about impossible to negotiate. It just gets more tangled, and if you do cut it the wire springs back all over the place. He said infantrymen would get completely stuck in the wire then picked off like fish in a barrel; sometimes they couldn't even get the bodies out after the guys had been killed."

I nodded. "I heard it's like this on all the beaches around the coast. It's like we've got a moat, and a barbed wire fence, and then all of England stuck inside."

"So how do we get in?" Charlie chimed in.

"In a lorry," said Graham.

"In a what?" Charlie and I replied together.

"A truck."

"How?"

"Don't you see them?" Graham pointed. "Down there, all lined up outside the main gate?"

"Looks like there's a lot of action," I said. "Something big must be going on."

"Exactly why we need to take a look," Graham responded. "But I've been watching. It usually takes about two or three minutes for each vehicle to get in and out of the guard post once they've arrived. Well, that's when we hop in the back. It should be easy."

I wasn't so sure. "What if we get caught?"

"We say sorry," he laughed. "Look, we're just kids, Henry. What are they going to do, shoot us?" He sounded so convincing I really couldn't argue. They were, after all, our soldiers.

"It's not like we're going to be sneaking into some enemy camp," Graham continued. "These are the good guys."

"So what are we waiting for?" I said. "Let's go."

We wheeled our bikes through the remainder of the gardens to the top of the steep road that leads down to the harbor. "The Road of Remembrance" runs parallel with the line of the cliffs, dropping a hundred fifty feet or so in just a quarter mile.

The road got its name because of the troops, thousands of them, who marched down the hill – in rank and file – to board the ships that took them to France and Belgium between 1914 and 1918. At the time it was known as *The Slope*, and the soldiers were ordered to "step short," in anticipation of the steep gradient.

Most of the men who marched down *The Slope* fought in the trenches of the Western Front, the infamous "War of Attrition." Not many of them ever made it home again.

"My mum's oldest brother ran away from home in the last war," I said. "He lied about his age and he walked down this hill with other kids who had lied about their ages, and the rest who were mostly only seventeen and eighteen anyway..."

"Where did he fight?" Charlie wanted to know.

"Belgium mainly," I said. "Nobody knew too much about how things went for him. Not until Flanders."

"Your uncle fought at Flanders?"

"Yep. Anyway, that's where they say he died. It's also known as the *Second Battle of Ypres*."

"Man..."

Flying down the hill at top speed was always a lot of fun. Although Charlie still clearly remembered his spectacular wreck from a couple of years back – the one that put him in the hospital for a few days.

"That's what you get if you run your bike into the back of a bus at twenty miles per hour," he used to joke.

But we thought better of such a spectacular descent as soon as we saw a red-faced policeman huffing and puffing a third of the way up. Instead, we took the pathway to the left that led to the back of the old graveyard behind St. Mary & St. Eanswythe, the historic parish church.

It always seemed like a complete change of worlds whenever we walked up the narrow path to the lush green churchyard. Honeysuckle vines draped the wobbly gate at the entrance, drenching the scene with a sweet, sticky fragrance. Cracked and mildewed tombstones dated back several hundred years, and were surrounded by well-kept lawns. The church itself had settled over the centuries, blending with a quiet kind of dignity into the ambiance of the oldest section of our town.

Our school routinely used the church building for special occasions, so we had attended a few services there. The whole place had the same musty, broken-down quality that characterized my great aunts. Both the church and my aunts appeared ready to keel over at any minute, as if whatever had contributed to sustaining them in terms of life had long since drained away. If my aunts had one foot in the graveyard, then the church had several. Most if its activity was buried there, along with the decaying saints. It was kind of sad, really, on both counts.

By the time we emerged into the narrow alleyways beyond the churchyard, it felt as if the years had been rolled back and we were experiencing the Folkestone of the late nineteenth century. Small shops and timeworn offices stood wedged between Elizabethan era houses that seemed to lean in a variety of directions. The cobblestoned streets were almost too narrow for even one vehicle to negotiate. We mounted our bikes and rode with caution, using our brakes all the way around.

A couple of tight turns brought us to the cobblestoned Old High Street that plummeted steeply down to Folkestone's inner harbor. "Let's go on down this way," I called to Graham and Charlie.

"Wait," Charlie said, pausing at the top of the hill while looking around at the empty street, "something feels wrong."

"What do you mean?" Graham replied as we dismounted to walk our bikes more safely down the precipitous incline. "Other than the fact that we're probably up to our eyeballs in serious trouble!"

"It's too quiet," Charlie replied. "At this time of the year the old part of town is usually thick with people on holiday. But there's hardly a person to be seen."

Graham laughed. "So who would come to sunny Folkestone for a seaside holiday when Hitler might drop a shell on your sandcastle, or have an invasion spoil your picnic! If, that is, you could find a beach without a dozen rolls of barbed wire in the first place."

"Exactly," I said. "But Charlie's right. This does feel kind of eerie."

It wasn't as if the town was deserted, abandoned, or hollow, or like it was inhabited by phantoms. It was something more real, and consequently more alarming. The street didn't have the regular buzz about it, the crowds, the life, and the noise we'd come to associate with this time of the year.

Gone totally was the cosmopolitan flavor brought by the influx of continental visitors who constantly crowded our town center. Somewhere, there was always the sound of an enthusiastic, "Bonjour!" We were used to hearing the chatter of French, the lilt of Italian, and the echo of German. But now the thought of hearing anyone talking in German had become chilling.

"What are you frowning about, Bradley?" Graham had caught the faraway look in my eyes. He poked me back to the present by calling my name.

"I'm just thinking," I said. And I shuddered involuntarily as I almost audibly heard the clatter of jackboots echoing on the cobblestone, and the retort of harsh commands in the air; I could practically see the residue of fear in the faces of innocent people....

"Whatever it is, it'll never happen," Charlie said confidently, as if he could read my mind. Which, unnervingly often, I really think he could.

"Right," I said as we reached the bottom of the steep hill, where Old High Street intersected with Tontine Street, and where a short turn to the right led directly down to the sheltered inner fishing harbor. "Let's chain our bikes to the bench here. We'll lay low and watch for a few minutes. We should be able to get a good look at what's going on."

"Sounds like a plan," Graham murmured, looking around intently like some kind of famous spy on the run from the authorities, gauging the risk.

It was always that way with my friends, everything a kind of a game, pushing back against the threat of growing up, not shirking responsibility so much as feeling the gravitational pull of our childhood asking for a little more time, a little less reality, a little more breathing room. But it was 1940, there was a war on, and we were teetering on the edge of a precipice. Looking back, I think we understood that. I think that's why we went so far as we did.

Graham pulled off his backpack and started digging around. "Anyone want something to eat?"

CHAPTER FIVE

Espionage Anyone?

We looked around carefully, amped up with expectation, wondering exactly what we were going to do next. We had made it to the bottom of the steep cobblestoned street free and clear – undetected so far as we knew, and success was making us bold. The gate to the restricted area stood just around the corner, and we found ourselves literally on the edge of following through - maybe. But would we actually do anything other than watch and plan? Our next move would be telling.

Most of the people we could see milling around were moving with a sense of purpose. This close to the docks, the comings and goings were clearly focused on specific tasks. There were no tourists, no recreational walkers, and no casual shoppers. There was no wandering around with all the time in the world and nothing urgent to attend to. We felt conspicuous, but at the same time invisible. We weren't on anyone's radar, so we were beginning to understand that, quite likely and if we were lucky, we simply didn't register.

Just then a wonderful smell wafted our way. Almost exactly on cue, all three of us turned toward the fish and chip shop that stood across the road and a couple of doors down on Tontine Street. "Can't you just taste it?" Charlie's eyes glazed over with desire.

"Haddock and chips for three," Graham said. "No, make it four, I could eat two helpings." Then he began to stand up. "Hold me back, mates, it's almost more than I can stand."

"Wait a minute," I said, grabbing at Graham's sleeve as a small army truck came careening around the corner from the harbor entrance. The driver pulled up outside the fish and chip shop with a screech of rubber. "I think this is our chance. Let's go."

A uniformed man climbed out of the truck with a big cardboard box. He hurried through the door under the "OPEN" sign, yelling a cheery greeting to the proprietor. The street was momentarily empty, so we crossed the road quickly, climbed carefully into the back of the army vehicle, pulled the tarpaulin cover over us, and sat in the semi-darkness, still as could be, shaking, hardly daring to breath, wondering what on earth had we gotten ourselves into.

"What do we do now?" hissed Charlie. He was already having second thoughts.

"We just wait and see," Graham said, a big grin spreading over his face. "Anything could happen. That's the point!" He jabbed me with his elbow. "We're having fun now. Right?"

"Right...." I wasn't quite convinced, but I had to admit that my adrenalin was flowing and I was open to the possibilities.

"Everyone quiet," I said. "Someone's coming."

It was the driver.

"All right then. Thanks mate. Right you are. Cheerio then." His raw Kentish accent featured a clipped barrage of dropped consonants and short, purposeful syllables. He took his leave of the merchant, opened the front door, threw his divine smelling load of fish and chips onto the passenger seat, and jammed the vehicle into gear. We were instantly deposited into a heap on the floorboards behind him.

"He's going to kill us before we can even get in the gate," I whispered to Graham.

"Just hold on tight," he laughed. Fortunately the old motor was so loud and the whole thing shook and grated so much between the gears that we were in no danger of being overheard.

"It feels like we're going up Tontine Street, away from the harbor," Charlie said.

"He's probably just driving around the block because this old jalopy is too much trouble to crunch into reverse," suggested Graham. Graham knew about such things because his dad raced cars, sold cars, and ran a garage up in Cheriton. He was always helping his dad tinker with repairs.

A sudden swerve to the left suggested Graham was accurate in his analysis.

"Oh no!" I exclaimed as we all slid back again, pressed against the tailgate. "Now we're going up the hill toward Rendezvous Street. We'd better hold onto something tight, because I think he's going to try to bounce this bucket of bolts down the old High Street."

Another sudden swerve to the left confirmed my suspicions, and we hurtled down one more connecting road before, hearts in mouths, plunging down the same steep, narrow, hill we had only a few minutes previously negotiated by carefully walking our bikes.

Charlie's face turned completely white. "I think the driver is some kind of deranged lunatic," he said between clenched teeth.

"How on earth is he going to stop this thing when we get to the bottom?"

Even as the words were coming out of Charlie's mouth, we felt our insides being rearranged as the truck screeched to an unscheduled halt, a lengthy skid preceding the complete stop. A paragraph or so of ripe army language flowed out of the cab, directed at the individual who had obviously been in the way.

Then, as the driver jerked the truck out into the road again, we heard an elderly lady yell a distinct, "Up yours too, soldier boy!" in the general direction of our departing vehicle.

Thankfully, the two or three bends in the road that led to the harbor were taken with less bravado. Our driver waited in line for an authorized entry while we huddled under the loose canvas, still as could be, wondering what would happen if someone decided to open the back and take a look.

"He's moving forward again," Charlie whispered. "Someone's coming up to the truck."

"Fish and chips for the officers," the driver called out.

"Right you are. Got some for me then?" the sentry hollered back.

"Not on your life, mate. There's none of this 'ere grub for the likes of us."

"Take more than a bloomin' war for that to 'appen. On you go then."

"Cheers, mate."

I looked at the others. We all grinned.

"We're in."

"Now what?"

"Now we see where exactly it is that our kind chauffeur is going to take us," Graham explained, as if he had every detail figured out in his master plan. "Then we hop out, we take a good look around, and we do whatever we want. Personally, I'd like to see what kind of specialized equipment the Royal Navy has stowed away here."

It sounded like a fine scheme to me.

The moment the truck parked, the driver jumped out with his prized cargo of fish and chips. We immediately climbed out the back and scurried behind some adjacent railroad cars.

"Okay then," Graham said. "Where do you want to go first?"

"How about around the side here, and out onto the jetty," I suggested. "We could take a closer look at any ships they have parked alongside."

"Great idea," Graham agreed. "These rail tracks look like they lead all the way past the warehouses and up to the loading areas. Let's follow them on in."

"Right," I said.

We began to pick our way carefully along the stationary train, the English Channel on one side and a row of boxcars on the other.

"This is too easy," I said to Charlie, who constantly had his guard up, looking in front, then behind, and off to the sides like a spooked rabbit. "I haven't even seen one single person in uniform since we got in."

"That's because we're so good at this," Graham laughed. "Maybe they should hire us for professional spies, and we could parachute into Germany to get secrets."

Graham always threw out great ideas that sounded like they'd make terrific stories for the adventure magazines and comic books we would read sometimes, when we were supposed to be taking care of our homework.

"I can see it now," Graham announced grandly. "The editors would put up huge headlines in *The Times*, and *The Daily Mail*:

'King George decorates schoolboy heroes with the Order of the British Empire.'"

"Right you are," a deep voice added to our conversation from directly behind where we were standing. "After I'm through with you they'll have to be awarded posthumously!"

We spun around, startled, unable to move, like deer caught in the headlights. I think my heart actually stopped for a moment.

It was our driver.

"Well, well, well. What 'ave we 'ere?"

He put one of his big hands on my shoulder and motioned for Graham and Charlie to follow. This wasn't meant to happen. At least it wasn't in our meticulously detailed plans, such as they were.

Derek Maul

CHAPTER SIX

Truth and Consequences

"What am I expected to do with you, Henry? Just what can I possibly do in response to some idiotic fool stunt like this? Can you come up with an answer to that, Henry? Well? Or are you just going to stare at the floor like you didn't see this coming?"

Of course my father didn't really want an answer. And I was smart enough – at least in that instance - not to try. But he kept on pushing.

"What were you thinking?" he said, looking almost like I had intentionally hurt him in some way. "Or were you even thinking at all? Schoolboy heroes? Medals? Spies? Are you mad? Don't you know there's a real war on? People are fighting and getting killed just a few miles away, while you and your friends are playing the fool!"

By now the emerging story of Dunkirk was beginning to come into focus – but not the scope of the operation. Of course we had

53

no clue an operation of any kind was already underway. Now dad was on the warpath for sure.

"Are you listening to me, Henry? Well are you? I expect your full attention when I'm trying to talk to you..." His voice was creeping up in volume.

"You're not talking to me," I pointed out unreasonably. "You're yelling at me."

I tried not to scowl, but the feeling overwhelmed me, and I fought hard – but not hard enough - to avoid getting sucked into the vortex of negative energy that was beginning to build, and expand, and then pressurize, in the small space between us.

"Will you ever learn not to talk back, young man?" My father was shaking his head as if to add disdain. "I think this is a prime opportunity for you to keep a lid on your smart remarks. I hope you realize how embarrassing this is..."

And there it was – bingo! We'd reached the bottom line in short order, right there. Everything ultimately had to reflect back on "the doctor" and his precious reputation. I could be run over by a truck and the first consideration would have been had I made too much of a mess on the sidewalk? I wouldn't want to embarrass Mr. Upstanding in the Community.

If I closed my eyes – and I must admit that I probably did – it could have been either my father or the headmaster of our school, Mr. Bryan, working themselves up into such a furious frenzy, flecks of white appearing at the corners of their mouths, veins standing out on their foreheads, knuckles white as their fists clenched in rage.

In my mind my two nemeses were virtually interchangeable. There was – typically - a predictable pattern, and here things were, ramping up right on schedule.

"Look at me, boy. I said you, boy. I said look at me...." He was getting louder. "And don't give me any of that insolent smirk you're so good at putting all over your face at a time like this...."

My dad, our esteemed headmaster. Dr. Bradley, Mr. Bryan. To my admittedly prejudiced point of view both of them were essentially the same. The conversation always started out mildly enough, with not so much of the yelling, not so much in the way of raised voices, no rapid descent into insults, at least not right away. But then the conflict always seemed to build into itself, gaining momentum. My father was actually quite adept at working himself up into his idea of "righteous" indignation, till – eventually - he became seriously incensed. He engineered it, he cultivated it, he finessed the process. The longer he talked at me, the louder he got. The more he yelled, the more furious he became.

By the time we were a couple of minutes into this kind of interaction my father would be convinced that it had been me, exclusively, who had deliberately and maliciously made him angry. Not only that, but once he had his mind made up in a situation that involved anger and blame, well, he was not going to back down at all, not ever.

To be clear, I'm not disputing the fact that I was completely out of line. Fact is, skipping school and sneaking onto a secure military establishment was beyond dumb. Our jaunt was the most serious misconduct I had ever been involved in. Quite frankly, looking back, our timing could not have been any worse.

But let's face it – how were we to know that the whole entire British army was on the edge of complete collapse?

No one told me, or Graham, or Charlie, that the Admiralty was already involved in organizing desperate operations to remove service personnel, under heavy fire, from the beach at Dunkirk, across the English Channel and a little way east along the Belgium coast.

And we might have approached things differently had we known that the exact harbor we were sneaking into had a key role to play in an effort that – if things didn't go well – may well have marked the last gasp of a nation destined for defeat at the hands of the most evil dictator the world had ever known.

Other than all that....

Charlie, Graham, and yours truly just happened to sneak into a critical port that was gearing up to support the massive evacuation at Dunkirk. Tens of thousands of lives were on the line, and there we were, playing our fantasy espionage games and getting in the way.

Breaking into a vital naval installation in the middle of "Operation Dynamo" may have been the single most brainless schoolboy prank in history. And it was certainly one of the clearest examples of "the wrong place at the wrong time" in my already checkered history as a kid.

Once we had been "arrested" and escorted to the guard house, the whole escapade quickly lost its carnival-like feeling of fun and games. However, it was still entirely up to my father how incensed and unreasonable he would become, and he sure could get that way in a hurry.

Headmaster Bryan tended to be more or less the same. Maybe they had been to the same school, I don't know. But, sitting there, closing my eyes, it could have been either one of them and it would have come out just about the same.

My dad continued the barrage. "I don't even know why I am wasting my time talking to you. Go straight to your room – I mean now – and you won't be coming out until I say you can come out. Is that completely clear?"

"Yes sir." I started to walk to the stairs, only too glad to get out of the living room. I hurried up the first flight with maybe too much of a spring in my step. But I should have known it wasn't going to be that easy. My dad started to follow me, still yelling. I guess he wasn't through.

"Have you listened to a word I've been saying to you? Do you have any idea how this affects my standing in this community? Has it ever occurred to you that your mother is seriously distressed regarding your ongoing unacceptable behavior?"

"Yes, I get it. But can I please just go on up to my room now?"

His face lit up with the possibility of drawing one more line in the sand. I could see the wheels turning.

"So you want to go to your room, do you? Well in that case no, you cannot go to your room. Come back here, boy. I HAVEN'T FINISHED TALKING TO YOU YET!!!"

My father's face was turning a deep crimson color. He was full bull shouting now.

"What I suggest to you, Henry, is that if you don't think that you need to behave, then you tell me just who it is that you think you are, young man…"

I kept on walking.

"Come back here! Where do you think you are going?"

"I'll be in my room, because that's where you sent me!" I called down over the banister at the top of the stairs. As I closed the door I could hear him stomping up after me. The whole house rumbled, or maybe cowered. I know he just wanted to yell.

I felt bad for my mother. I know she suffered terribly on account of my conflicts with my dad. It was pretty much for her sake I fought so hard not to get drawn into the shouting – although I could have done a lot better, way better. But it wasn't easy.

Usually she'd just sit there in the living room listening, as my dad became increasingly irate.

"Now dear..." mum would sometimes begin, trying to get involved. But my dad was always too angry, too full of himself, too righteous I guess to see that anyone else might have some constructive input. And she never pushed it, she never intervened, she never insisted that things go down any differently. I do so wish that she had.

My dad banged on my door, and I felt fortunate that he didn't try to force his way in. "Don't you come out of there until you're told to. Do you hear me?"

"Yes, I hear you," I said." Yes, sir."

*   *   *   *

I have to tell the truth, it wasn't only my father's remonstrations that left me feeling uptight and deeply troubled. For the first time since the outbreak of hostilities, the hard reality of what was beginning to happen - right there in my England - was settling in on all of us for the first time.

Until that incident, that particular moment when I had felt the large hand on my shoulder and we were unceremoniously ushered into the guardhouse, the entire build-up to war – as well as the potential for invasion - had held a surreal quality. It never entered our minds that this darkening situation was anything so directly connected to us. I think it was true for all of us, and most especially for me.

Let's face it, I had led a sheltered life my first fifteen-plus years. The greater happenings of the world at large had never intruded on the stream of conscious experience that was my life - the small world I inhabited with my close friends.

We read the newspapers, yes, and we occasionally got our hands on some of the sleazier magazines that sensationalized crime, sex, war, sports, and espionage. But we lived with relative immunity in a benign, innocent, privileged world that had been constructed to protect kids like us from anything foreign to our fairytale existence.

Ours was a way of life designed by the lords of British privilege, and history, and the sense of separation we felt from the rest of the world. It was a way of life that – right in front of my eyes - was now being fundamentally threatened.

Concentration camps, conquest, refugees, beatings, destruction of property, political killings, brute squads, bombs, trial without the benefit of due process, detention without a hearing - these features all belonged to other worlds, other nations, other peoples. A lot of common British sentiment didn't even allow that we were actually part of Europe. Instead, we viewed ourselves as a favored appendage, something a cut above, floating off the northwest corner of a continent that earned mixed reviews. We were immune, therefore, to the troublesome issues that plagued our neighbors.

My faith in our invulnerability was shaken to the core, and the hard realization that none of this was make-believe anymore had the effect of a hard punch to the stomach. When real soldiers in real uniforms failed to crack a single smile at our "boyish pranks," we couldn't ignore the truth of it any longer. Now we had no choice but to take note.

"In the last war," a gruff military policeman lectured us while we were waiting for our parents the day we were caught at the harbor, "I personally ran my bayonet right through the gullet of one young whippersnapper just about your age."

We sat upright, our mouths opening and closing like fish.

"Do you think that was fun?" the M.P. whispered, leaning in so close we could smell the stale cigarette smoke on his breath. "Do you think that's an image I want stuck in my head for the rest of my days? Gawd... it was the single most horrific moment of my life. Before he died, the kid cried out for his mummy. What are you, sixteen?"

"Almost," I replied, sick to my stomach. "Charlie and Graham here just turned."

"Right you are," he continued. "My point is this isn't any kind of a game, and no one appreciates people who make fun of something this serious."

The toughened veteran pushed his hard face a little closer in. "Are we clear on this point?"

"Yes, sir."

*   *   *   *

The next day when we arrived at school we were all invited to the headmaster's office, right after morning assembly. Fortunately we had to wait a few minutes before we were called in. We had time to put our heads together and talk things over. Maybe we could put on some kind of a united front and do something to avoid the kind of major trouble we knew we probably deserved.

"What did your parents dish out, Graham?" I asked. Mr. Fern was no pushover. His dad was hard but fair, and tended to be a lot calmer than mine.

"The usual stuff. Straight home from school for a couple of weeks. No friends over. Letters of apology to Mr. Bryan and the army people. Extra work with dad at the garage every day until my restriction is over."

"Charlie?"

"Well, my mum cried, that was probably the worst. My dad got all huffy and went on about the King, trustworthiness, honor, God, and all that stuff. Apart from that it was pretty much the same package as Graham. You?"

"I still don't really know. My dad hasn't calmed down long enough to actually do anything. My mum won't talk about it. I think she's too scared it'll get Dr. Doom going again."

"Dr. Doom!" Graham exclaimed. "I like that."

Mr. Bryan opened his study door, signaling us all in together, which was a good sign. Any time he dealt with students in a group it meant he didn't have either the time or the inclination to yell at us all individually.

It was obvious our headmaster was preoccupied with other, more weighty, concerns, because he immediately launched into a lecture that was almost the exact twin of my father's.

He skipped the usual preamble, fast-forwarding directly to the yelling. This rant came complete with red face, wild hand gestures, sticking out veins, and – eventually - white froth around the corners of his mouth. Plus - of course - the lack of real interest in anything we might have to say.

But we could tell Mr. Bryan's heart really wasn't in it. All the punishment amounted to, after all was said and done, was two weeks of detention after school, the threat of a beating, and a thousand lines each: "I will not discredit my school and embarrass my family." Annoying, yes, but of no real consequence in reality.

We discussed the situation later that day at school lunch – a disgusting plate full of something half warm and creamy, along with soggy vegetables.

"I envy you your father, Graham," I said.

"Why's that, Henry? My dad can be pretty hard sometimes."

"Well, at least I think you know where you stand with him. His consequences tend to bring you closer, not drive you apart. When he's angry it actually seems to make sense. Then there's one other big thing."

"What?"

"I get the idea that he respects you."

Graham looked at me, not really understanding. "Well it's mutual. Isn't it always?"

I smiled to myself, but not really. "Well, whatever it is, you're certainly right that it's mutual."

I felt like I wanted to cry.

CHAPTER SEVEN

Everything We'd Feared, and More

The letter we'd all been dreading came home the very next day. It was from my school, and it was the worst possible scenario in a nutshell. It was the evacuation.

Dear parent(s): Due to the increasing threat of invasion, and the frequent incidents of shelling all along the coast, measures are being taken to ensure the safety of all our children. To that end, evacuation proceedings will begin this coming Sunday, June 2nd, leaving from Platform One at Folkestone West railway station. School staff will be accompanying the boys, as we shall do our best to continue to meet as a school once we are relocated. Please gather at the assembly hall promptly at 8:15 in the morning. It is hoped that information regarding destination and host families will be forthcoming at that time.

To me the real meaning read a little more simply: *"Dear Dr. and Mrs. Bradley. Your child is a complete idiot. We still can't believe he tried to mess up the evacuation at Dunkirk. We strongly urge you to put him on a train and send him far, far away."*

All I could think about were the horror stories I'd heard regarding the confusion and uncertainty inherent in this process. Whole trainloads of children dumped at railroad stations in unknown destinations all over the country - maybe some miserable mining town, then getting picked through and sorted like so much produce at the grocery store. I'd heard about people taking home kids as free servants to do their dirty work, so they wouldn't have to. Brothers and sisters were often forced to split up and go to different homes. And there was no screening system in place designed to exclude mean people who might beat children for looking at them the wrong way.

Hosting was encouraged as "Patriotic Duty," and families didn't necessarily volunteer with enthusiasm. Participation was often imposed - arbitrary and mandatory. Then there were those who resented being told to take anyone in. Not to mention the crazy people, doing all sorts of nameless things to kids whose parents maybe didn't even know where they were....

But then I'd also heard stories (rumors) of poor children from the city ending up at some amazing manor house and getting breakfast in bed from the maid every day - bona fide fairytale stuff. There was also talk of horse riding, steak for dinner, clean clothes, big bathtubs, long walks in the country, and strawberries and cream at teatime every day.

Fact is I didn't want either end of the potential story. I wouldn't want to stay with King George and the Queen in the palace, and I certainly didn't want to end up in some coal mine digging dirt for ten hours a day and being smacked around for my trouble. I wanted my friends, and my town, and even my school. I wanted to keep my life, and for nothing to ever change.

So after I got home I waited around for either my mum or my dad to say something, anything. My mother had left the house suddenly and without comment, right after I'd biked home with the letter at the end of lunchtime. I went back to school for the afternoon, and she went directly to dad's office.

"You know we talk about anything important together before we make a decision or say anything to you," my mum always said, anytime there was the potential for differing views. It sounded like a good system, although I suspected it was a farce, the truth more along the lines of my mother having to ask my dad first because it would eventually come down to him anyway. I wondered why they even bothered pretending.

This time the waiting was just about killing me. So, around ten minutes into our evening meal, I decided to break the ice.

"Well I'm glad I won't have to go live with some host family in a far-away town," I said optimistically, watching intently for a reaction while slurping my second cup of tea.

My mother dropped her spoon on the saucer with a loud clang that echoed around the room. The sound was amplified by the total silence that followed. There was nothing, nada, crickets. All I could hear was the ticking of the big grandfather clock in the hallway.

So I tried an alternate approach. "I know there are some boys whose parents have already told them they won't have to go anywhere," I ventured. Although I was totally making it up – I really didn't know anything of the sort.

"Anyway, Mum" – and I smiled at her with as much manipulative devotion as I could muster – "you know I couldn't possibly survive without your Yorkshire pudding."

My poor mother looked like she was going to burst into tears at any minute. She held a small handkerchief poised, expectantly, halfway to her face, sniffing intermittently. The old clock started to chime the hour. I shifted uneasily in my chair.

"Ahem…," my dad always cleared his throat before he had something he thought was important to say. He took another sip of his tea, and then leaned back in his overstuffed chair. "I don't want to be the one responsible for leaving my son in harm's way if one of those bombs comes in through our living room window."

"What?" A heavy red haze seemed to materialize, blurring my vison and threatening to close in all around me.

"The shelling. Yes, that's right," my father stuttered, hesitantly. "There have been several serious incidents recently. Plus the very real possibility of invasion, now that the Expeditionary Force seems to have failed in its task."

He seemed to be checking off the items one at a time in his mind. "Additionally, you know very well the government would not go to all this trouble of organizing and recommending…"

The air in the room seemed to thicken. My father's words just started to blend in with the background. I didn't want to listen to any of his justifications. It was all nothing more than a boatload of congealed crap. There was no way to make something like this sound reasonable. Not any more than there was a way to make armies of grown men fighting each other - literally to the death - sound anything other than the absurdity it was.

It certainly didn't sound anything but consummately unfair to a boy whose whole life was spread all around him in the hills and cliffs and fields and beaches of the south of England. Not to a boy who understood security as his intimate knowledge of the roads and streets and paths that made up his town. Not to a boy who really needed a father right now… even though everything about our relationship seemed to be pushing us farther apart.

I just couldn't believe it. They were going to send me away. It was obvious my parents had already made up their minds. Their only child, sent out of town for who knows how long? It didn't matter to me that just about every other kid in Folkestone would be leaving, not to mention a lot of the adults too.

I couldn't take this in from any reference point of reason, so I started to panic: "Please don't make me go. I'll hate it, you know I will."

My mother started to cry, my dad held her hand. Not so much for comfort as to stop her from running out of the room.

"We are very clear on this, Henry. We talked it though extensively at my office this afternoon, and we've been thinking about this eventuality for several weeks. Don't make the situation more difficult for your mother than it already is. We all have to do our best now. There's a war on - stiff upper lip and all that."

My father sounded like one of those public service messages on the radio.

*　　　　*　　　　*　　　　*

"I know exactly why he's doing it," I explained to Graham at lunch in the cafeteria the next day.

"He? Or they?" Charlie interrupted.

"He, definitely." I sounded like I was trying to convince myself as much as them.

"My mum would never make me go to some stupid town stuck in the middle of who knows where. Somewhere the government supposedly imagines we'll be safe. I know why he's going along with it. It's so convenient, just an easy excuse to get me out of the way so I don't bother him anymore, so I won't embarrass his precious reputation..." I was getting up a full head of steam. "So I won't disappoint him, so I won't so obviously get in the way of his boring little life, so...."

Frustrated, I slammed my cup down to emphasize my point. Seemingly effortlessly, a beautifully formed spout of water jumped about two feet into the air, turned gracefully to the left, and landed on the table with a splash, partially soaking Graham's gooseberry pie.

"Thanks a lot, Bradley," he laughed. "I'll spare you the pie in the face routine because I know you're upset." Graham could be surprisingly sensitive at times. "Hey, remember how much trouble you got into with your water glass back in elementary school?"

I had to smile. "Well at least it was empty that time. Except that's not what *'Old Three Trees'* told the headmaster!"

"'This boy...'" I could still do a fair imitation of her grating, irritating, high-pitched voice; "'This boy threw a glass full of water all over the girls. Mr. Rogers (the headmaster), this kind of behavior cannot be tolerated in our school. I want to see that he is punished, and I expect that you punish him severely.'"

Charlie and Graham were shaking with laughter. "All that," Graham said, "for sliding an empty glass no more than a couple of inches down the table."

"All that for being a boy," Charlie chimed in, "and for not being one of her precious, darling, do-no-wrong girls."

"That's right," I said. "The truth wouldn't have helped, though, because Mr. Rogers was more afraid of her than I was. He suspended me from school lunches for the rest of the term, just so she wouldn't yell at him anymore."

Graham was still laughing. "If we even looked at a girl wrong she was all over us. Things were simple for *Old Three Trees:* girls were little angels and all the boys – especially us – were nothing but bad."

Charlie cleared his throat loudly. "I have to go too."

Things suddenly got quiet again. The brief distraction was over, and our attention had to turn back to the difficult things we were all facing. I had failed to notice, but Charlie hadn't been talking all that much up to this point.

"Maybe we can all stay somewhere together," Charlie said, "some huge, cool estate with rich people, out in the country! But I don't feel so badly as you do, Henry. I really believe my parents are scared to death that something bad is going to happen to me if we stay here."

"What about Rose?" Rose was Charlie's sister. She was three years younger, exceptionally cute, and lots of fun. She'd nurtured an obvious crush on me ever since I could remember.

"Scotland," Charlie said. "We have an aunt in Inverness willing to take her in. But it's just her. Anyway, I'm glad I'm not going up there. There's nothing to do six months out of the year, plus it's so cold. I think I'd die of boredom, or winter – or maybe both."

"So I wonder where exactly we'll all be shipped off to," I added. "I sure as heck hope it isn't one of those miserable mining towns, where everyone walks around covered in soot and looking depressed all day."

Now it was Graham's turn to look uneasy. "That's going to have to be, 'where are *you* going?' not 'where are *we* going,'" he said quietly.

Charlie and I looked at him.

"What?" I asked.

"Graham?" Charlie queried.

"My parents have decided to keep me at home," Graham explained. "My dad says he can't afford to lose my help around the garage, and he's extra busy with a lot of work on the side to help the army vehicles keep rolling. Plus they both said they aren't nearly ready to see me leave."

"Damn," Charlie breathed.

"You lucky dog," I chimed in.

"Maybe not so lucky that I won't have my best friends," Graham responded. "I mean, who will be here to get me into trouble all the time? And I don't know if you two morons know how to take care of yourselves?"

"Let's not get too sentimental here," I said.

"Let's not forget what's important either," replied Graham.

"No," I looked him straight in the eye, "I don't think I ever will."

CHAPTER EIGHT

All Aboard for the Mystery Tour

The plot of the story we were living in had progressed extremely quickly, accelerating over the short week that had rushed headlong and out of control since the three of us sat on the hilltop, daring Hitler to take us on. To tell the truth, it was like an avalanche, precipitous, constantly gaining momentum. Suddenly it was June, the "Phony War" was well and truly over, and we couldn't go on pretending anymore that nothing bad was going to happen on our side of the English Channel.

After a series of frustrating setbacks in northern Europe, the entire Allied army had to turn around and come home. In fact, between May 26 and June 4 (the full extent of Operation Dynamo, later remembered as The Miracle of Dunkirk), three hundred forty thousand Allied troops had been rescued from the beaches at Dunkirk, all while being shot, bombed, strafed, shelled, harassed, and generally attacked by the German army.

Over eight hundred fifty vessels, all the way from ships the size
of destroyers to the tiniest of fishing boats, had gone back and
forth across the English Channel (the *Pas-de-Calais* as the French
called it), carrying as many stranded soldiers as possible.

Not only were the expeditionary forces compelled to leave all
of the equipment behind, but hundreds of boats were lost too. Still,
the evacuation was a success of historic proportions. The calm
weather - lasting an unprecedented number of consecutive days -
was not only unusual, but described as "a miracle" by people who
weren't even religious. Because of the singular conditions,
everyone who had a craft of any kind was able to make their way
over and be of some help. It was the biggest, and most successful,
beach exodus in history.

All things considered, Germany now held all the cards. The
British forces were in complete disarray. It certainly looked as if
our little island was a sitting duck, with people going so far as to
describe this as "England's darkest hour." It was like our whole
country was stuck in a roll of razor wire, unable to wriggle free,
waiting for the end to come.

I was even beginning to understand a little more about why my
parents were so anxious to get me out of town.

*   *   *   *

The simplest explanation – and the one that made sense - is that
my school was being evacuated because Adolph Hitler was on the
verge of pressing his advantage for an invasion. We were going to
see increased shelling from German positions in France (the
barrage had already started), there was the certainty of extended
air raids (it was just a matter of time), and then the Nazi forces
were going to land on the beaches (not "if" but "when").

The invasion was coming - it wasn't a question so much as a looming inevitability, and there was – seemingly – nothing that could be done to prevent it.

Every evening our little family huddled around the radio to hear the latest news. It had been frightening enough to realize that the expeditionary forces had been pushed back to the English Channel so easily. Then many people were close to panic when they understood hundreds of thousands of soldiers were hemmed in on a beach in Belgium, only fifteen miles long. But to witness, firsthand, the complete capitulation of an army? Now that was almost too much.

I clearly remember hearing the call for craft - "boats of any kind" - go out over the radio. It was the day after our fiasco down at the harbor, and we all understood the sense of desperation that was impossible to mask. We felt helpless to do anything to aid a lost army almost within sight of home. And, for those few days before we kids were scheduled to leave Folkestone by train, the vision of total collapse was sitting right there on the horizon.

Who was to know the Nazis would fail to follow the retreating army right across the English Channel without pause, immediately annihilating defenses at the very moment our country was so severely compromised? We could visualize the bloody fighting in the streets of our town, and in the fields and on the hills around us. It looked like the destruction of life as we knew it.

However, and in contrast, my friends and I also witnessed the classic and comforting mood of British bull-doggery. While fear may have had its moments, it had also been eight hundred seventy-four years since any kind of invading army had successfully landed on and held an English beach.

A popular song expressed the sentiment of British resistance this way: "Who do you think you are kidding, Mr. Hitler, if you think we're on the run?" English people owned a fierce sense of determination that, even if the worst case scenario unfolded (and by any accounting, this was pretty bad), the English spirit of "making do," the spirit of "keep calm and carry on," would include ferocious resistance, right along with making everyone strong cups of tea and maintaining our dignity in the face of hard times.

$$* \qquad * \qquad * \qquad *$$

Eventually, Sunday morning came and we had to go. The noise and bustle in our school assembly hall was just about as confusing as a three ring circus. Approximately four hundred boys, all with brown labels attached to their jackets, featuring name, address, school, and an identity number.

There were scores of parents too, plus twenty or so teachers, all jostling in close proximity, all trying to find the right place to meet up with their assigned cluster of friends and classmates.

We were travelling by homeroom. My teacher, Mr. Thomas, had picked a place close to the main doors, and we were instructed to stick to him like glue until we made it to the final destination. The general idea was to set up a functioning school community in another town, sharing facilities via some kind of creative schedule, while trying to keep our lives as close to normal as possible.

Even the best laid plans, though, were subject to change, because there was not one person in that room who even knew where we were going, when the invasion would come, if England would be successfully defended, or when – and even if - we might expect to come home.

Eventually, by around 8:30, twenty distinct groupings had emerged around the assigned teachers. Our headmaster went to the podium to answer questions and give out last minute instructions. He looked more than a little flustered.

"No, I'm sorry," Mr. Bryan said for maybe the tenth time in as many minutes, "we do not yet have information regarding where it is that our students are going. They will find out when they get there – and that applies to school officials too. Those of us who stay behind will find out later. All the boys will be encouraged to write letters to their parents, immediately upon arrival, with any and all pertinent details. But no one is going to know anything definitive until they are settled in with their host families…

"These are," headmaster Bryan continued, in an effort to match his rhetoric to the historical nature of the moment, "trying times. With the fall of France, and the tragedy of Dunkirk, we do not know what to expect. We hold here with these dear boys a unique trust…" he sucked his breath in and drew himself up to his full five foot six inches, "… and I wish to assure all of the parents and friends here that we will do our utmost to prove worthy of that trust."

I had to admit that Mr. Bryan almost struck an impressive tone.

"I would like to say that this threat will pass quickly, and promise you that these dear ones will safely return to the bosom of their families very soon. But, until then," and here he raised his right hand in a dramatic flourish to go with the sentimental words, "we pledge our best for these youngsters and, yes, for England."

I elbowed Charlie. "What, is he running for Prime Minister?" I whispered. He tried not to giggle.

A small scattering of applause was offered for the headmaster's efforts, like the last few seconds of popcorn popping, more for conclusion than for content. And then it was suddenly time for us to go, to walk in our noisy classroom groups up to the station, and to board the waiting train.

"Would you like me to come up with you?" asked my mum.

"No. Thanks." I was afraid I might cry. "Let's say goodbye here."

My mother's handkerchief had hovered in midair for most of the past hour, affecting its usual crisis deployment mode, halfway between her pocket and her nose. I could tell that she was having trouble speaking. She was even having a hard time getting enough air.

"D... don't forget to brush your teeth," she stammered.

"And I'll write, first thing. I promise." I said.

All around us we could hear the sound of tearful goodbyes. Some fathers were there – brusque, gruff, putting on a brave face. It was mostly mothers, though, as the majority of the younger men had already been called up for military service.

My dad had excused himself at breakfast that morning, brandishing a busy schedule as evidence, claiming commitments to his patients. He limited himself to shaking my hand when I left the house, fending off my attempt at a hug with a friendly slap on the back.

"I love you, Dad," I had offered.

"Take care of yourself, son," was all he could manage in reply. "Try not to get into any trouble. Make your mother and me proud." Then he hastily retreated back into his study, leaving me feeling like we had passed by each other once again. So close, but yet so far. God, I hoped we would get another chance.

Suddenly my mum threw her arms around my neck and kissed me, wet, on the cheek. "I love you so very much, Henry," she cried.

"And I love you, Mum. Please don't be too sad. I hope you write to me about everything."

She had to almost pull herself away from me. Mum gave one last look through the sopping wet handkerchief, stuffed what turned out to be a last minute set of instructions and some extra cash in my pocket and, turning quickly away, hurried out the door. She was gone before I had a chance to wave.

I stood there with my grandfather's old travel suitcase in one hand, and my school satchel slung over a shoulder. Big tears stained my cheeks. I was almost unable to move. I didn't know when I would see her again. I suddenly felt overwhelmed by the whole rapid, devastating, turn of events.

*   *   *   *

I took half a step backward, and tripped over Charlie. My friend had just said goodbye to both his parents, with less fuss than me but with equal trauma. We kind of leaned on each other, and began walking with our group down Cheriton Road, as far as the crossover at Cherry Garden Avenue. It was just a short walk up the hill to Folkestone West train station, where the carriages were already waiting. The morning sun shone gently, and there was a warm breeze coming in from the sea.

"Keep up, boys," yelled Mr. Thomas, "There's a war on, you know."

Platform One was awash with the black and red of our school uniforms. Some parents had elected to continue the epic struggle to say goodbye all the way to the train, but - by and large - this was now exclusively a school occasion. We had started to revert to our role as students, looking to our teachers for cues, reinterpreting the day's events with a sense of schoolboy adventure.

"All aboard for the mystery tour," Charlie called out quietly, earning a handful of snickers from the closest boys, crowded like a herd of sheep as we waited for our next set of instructions.

The youngest age groups boarded first. Then Mr. Thomas, along with the French language teacher, Mr. Prater, led our "5th form" conglomeration (the equivalent of high school sophomores) on to the rickety old train.

"All the way to the front, boys," said Mr. Thomas. "Two of you to every three seats should be comfortable enough. Luggage up top. And, Bradley," here he took a long critical look at me for some reason, "try to keep your feet off the seats."

I raised one eyebrow in a question. "Sir?"

"You know…"

"Absolutely. Yes, sir."

We ended up being more crowded than Mr. Thomas had thought, as train space was at a premium in the war economy and with so many demands on the system. Some of the boys had to sit on their luggage, but we all managed to make ourselves fairly comfortable. I wondered where on earth we might be headed? Regardless of the destination, this could be just the beginning of a very long day.

"So where do you think we're going to end up, sir?" Charlie asked our teacher.

"We'll get a better idea after we change train stations in London," said Mr. Thomas. "I can guarantee one thing, though; we certainly won't be staying in the city."

*   *   *   *

We hadn't made our way any farther north than Ashford, just fifteen miles, when the train stopped halfway through the station.

Our carriages sat motionless for the best part of an hour, off in a siding, because some of the troop trains coming through had to be given priority.

One of the army trains was stuffed full with veterans from Dunkirk. We were both at a standstill, side by side, for several minutes. It was an odd juxtaposition, the very young and the prematurely old. We observed each other with mutual humanity and goodwill. The men in uniform were obviously weary. Some looked permanently horrified. Most of them were filthy. There were men covered in mud, despair, disappointment, and blood. The experience gave me chills.

The first few miles out of Folkestone had featured a hubbub of excited chatter echoing through the train – especially as we watched the familiar territory around our town begin to disappear. We were bound for an unknown destination, and all of us were – simultaneously - both anxious and excited.

Then, especially in light of what we saw at the station in Ashford, and by the time we reached the outskirts of London, a pensive stillness prevailed. Charlie and I looked out of the window as the train slowed to a crawl approaching the River Thames, and we wondered once again where we would be at the end of this day.

FOLKESTONE INTERVIEW – 1990

Henry got up from his deep leather chair for the first time in a long time, yawning expansively: the big clock on the coffeehouse wall read 4:45 in the afternoon.

"If I don't stretch my legs now I may never move again," he said.

Elizabeth finished penning a long sentence on her notepad, ending her thought with a flourish.

"I really don't want to stop the interview," she said. "But you have got to be more than completely jet-lagged from yesterday."

"I booked a bed and breakfast not far from here," he replied. "Let me get in a long walk and a good night's sleep, and I'll be more than ready to pick up the story in the morning. How about you?"

"I wouldn't miss it for the world," Elizabeth said; "I can't help myself, this story is pulling me in. Are you sure you're okay with all the time this is taking?"

"I'm just as interested in discovering what I'm going to say as you are!" Henry smiled. "I didn't fly here from America just to look at the view; I came because I need to hear this story myself. Just being in Folkestone is already helping me to pull out some of the details I thought I'd forgotten a long time ago."

He grabbed the reporter's hand with a sudden surge of conviction, as if needing to make the connection more concrete.

"I don't know how much time you have over the next few days," he said. "But what if we do the next part of the interview up on the hills? I could show you our old lookout point..."

"That would be amazing!" Elizabeth laughed. "But, please, no bikes for me, just a car ride and a short hike. How early can you be ready?"

* * * *

The year or the decade didn't matter. 1940? 1990? Regardless, the view from the hills behind the town was wondrous.

It was a clear, cool, morning with the visibility just about perfect. Henry could see changes, of course – popping out one at a time, like the multiplicity of stars that make themselves evident the longer you look into the night sky. Less open farmland, more housing developments, the sweep of a modern bypass running along the foot of the escarpment, a huge roundabout exactly where he'd once built an impressive treehouse with his friends, new factories under the shadow of Sugarloaf Hill, the unending expanse of equipment and construction supporting the massive Channel Tunnel project.

But the big picture was much the same: sitting in the same place, looking out toward the English Channel, the cliffs of Dover, the town he loved so well. Reclining there in the long grass, feeling the breeze, closing his eyes... Henry could sense the presence of his boyhood friends like it was yesterday. If he could just reach out they would be there, Charlie, Graham....

And he did. Henry kept his eyes closed, he drank in the fresh air, and – involuntarily - he reached out his hand. He could see them both, he felt them, viscerally. He sensed real emotion. And, to his great surprise, he cried.

CHAPTER NINE - 1940

Evacuated - "Destination Unknown"

Honestly, I felt confused as much as anything else, riding the slow train toward London, drifting along the tracks to some unknown destination, moving into a life that wasn't anything like the 1940 summer I had planned. Any notion that the war could ever possibly begin to get this serious had never even entered our minds.

To be fair, what Charlie, Graham, and I meant by "serious" was – more accurately - *anything inconvenient for us*. My friends and I still owned an egocentric sense of "we're too special" insularity when it came to the rest of the world. We were young, we were naïve, and we were protected. But the edges of our unrealistic world were beginning to fray.

We'd read reports about the terrible oppression in Europe, but we hadn't considered the possibility that it was our lives that might be turned upside down – at least not until our unplanned reality check down by the harbor. Of course, in Folkestone we had seen the barbed wire on the beaches, and we'd been aware of the "Home Guard" activity, and then there was the increased army presence around the port, and we had listened intently to all the radio reports.

But it hadn't been until we were handed the unwelcome news we were becoming "evacuees" that we had shown more than a nominal interest in the troubles of the wide world beyond us. Up until that moment we were completely immersed in our easy and sheltered life, the life we loved, the familiar life we were now being herded away from.

In just a few short days, everything had changed. The episode down at the docks, the fateful letter home from my school, and – in a kind of *coup de grâce* - the frightening repercussions surrounding the fate of the Allied forces on the beach at Dunkirk. Until then – and I'm not proud of this at all – not much of the war "over there" had seemed to be all that relevant, or all that real.

These were the thoughts that started crowding into my mind as we made less than "express" progress on our mystery rail journey to who-knew-where. Eventually, as we crossed the River Thames and our train rolled toward the huge terminus of Charing Cross station, Mr. Thomas stood up.

"Boys," he announced. "I have a new shilling for the first one of you able figure out which part of the country we're going to. If you know London well enough, then you will quickly guess which railway station we're headed for. Then, if you know your geography, you should be able to deduce which part of England it serves."

Charlie turned to me and started to name off the names of all the London terminus railway stations, rattling information off like he was an encyclopedia.

- "Victoria – that would take us back toward Canterbury."
- "Paddington – from there we'd be headed west."
- "Euston station serves Stratford, Chester, and all the way north to Glasgow."
- "Kings Cross handles everything through York and then Edinburgh."
- "Liverpool Street – let me think…"

"Cambridge and East Anglia?" I offered.

"That's right," Charlie nodded. "Then of course there's my favorite, Waterloo. Did you know it's the biggest rail terminal in England? If we went out from there we could end up anywhere from Salisbury to Cornwall and deep into the south-west coast."

"And we're already in Charing Cross station once we've finished crossing this bridge," I continued. "So that accounts for all the main stations in London. Charlie - I had no idea you knew that much about the railways. I'm almost impressed."

"Well, like my uncle Dave always says, 'If you're not going to learn your Three-R's, then you might as well know something about trains.'" He smiled. "Of course he's been unemployed most of his life!"

It took our teachers a few minutes to get us all onto the platform, organized, and then count heads to make sure nobody was left behind. Out on the street we had to load up several double-decker buses, and then get counted all over again. Our group ended up in the first bus away from the station, and as we pulled out, heading east along The Strand and up toward Fleet Street, Charlie and I knew immediately where we were going.

"Sir, sir," Charlie tugged at Mr. Thomas's sleeve.

"What is it, Green?" The teacher turned around in his seat.

"We're definitely headed toward Liverpool Street station. That means East Anglia. So I'm saying our destination is almost positively Cambridge, sir."

Charlie looked very pleased with himself. Mr. Thomas got out a piece of paper and carefully wrote something down.

"Well. Am I right, sir? Do I get the shilling?" My friend could barely contain himself.

"I don't know yet, Green," Mr. Thomas replied, offering a wary smile, an expression that revealed more than a little of the disquiet the adults must have been experiencing too.

"I'm writing down your prediction," he said, "and also the time – indeed you are the first. I guess we'll see if you're right whenever we get to wherever it is that we're going."

There was a long silence.

"You mean you really don't know, sir?" Several of the boys had stopped to listen in.

"That's right," Mr. Thomas sighed. "I really don't know where we are going."

"Wow!" Charlie exclaimed. "This really is a mystery tour..."

*   *   *   *

What with all the delays, the loading and unloading, and the repeated counting of squirming schoolboys, it was well into the afternoon before our train rolled slowly out of Liverpool Street station. We gathered speed as the train headed northeast toward to low country of East Anglia, the big fertile bulge of England that is covered with a network of dikes and drainage ditches, much like the famous tulip fields in Holland.

The city of Cambridge was built around the river Cam. It was, and still is, a picturesque university town that bustles around the colleges and chapels of the world-famous school. Our train approached the station at almost exactly three o'clock, easing in slowly, gradually coming to a halt, finally coming to a stop with a long *hiss* of steam. Immediately, all the boys around me started grabbing at their luggage in anticipation of the end of our long journey.

"Come on, Charlie, let's get our stuff," I said.

"Do you see anyone on the platform?" he asked.

"No." I shook my head.

"How about over there on the street?"

"Nope, not there, either." I could see where he was going with this.

"Then I think I was a little bit wrong with my guess. I don't think we're all the way there yet."

"But most of the boys are getting their stuff down," I argued. "Look, even some of the masters."

"Then most of them are going to fall over on their bums when we get going again," Charlie grinned.

Things went exactly as predicted. The train suddenly lurched forward, and a whole lot of people – including the often tightly wound Mr. Prater – ended up, involuntarily, down on the floor sitting on their luggage.

"Comfortable, sir?" Charlie ventured, with a little too much of a grin on his face, looking in the direction of the French language teacher.

"Funny, Green. Very funny...."

Then he muttered something in French that was at once both unintelligible and clearly understandable. He was not smiling.

About fifteen miles beyond Cambridge, the train stopped again. This time the sign on the platform would have read "Newmarket" if a sign had been there. But, as Mr. Thomas explained, "If anyone unfriendly drops in with their parachute, we don't want to make it too easy for them to find their way around."

In fact, and in communities all over England, road signs, town signs, and train station signs were being removed for just that purpose. The notion of potential invasion, parachuting spies, or hostile expeditionary forces, was getting a lot of attention. Things were tense, and leaving home like this was not making our apprehension any less pronounced.

"All right everyone, it looks like this is it." Mr. Thomas stuck his head back in the train after chatting with someone on the platform. "We need to assemble outside in the car park. Let's stay in our groups, and no lurking around."

Charlie and I stuck close. Mr. Thomas's group lined up near a low wall, and we sat together toward the back, having agreed to take a good long look at things before we committed ourselves to an uncertain situation. It was very obvious we were at the mercy of forces we could tell we had little to no control over.

At first glance it looked like we were going to have to listen to another long, tedious speech. A short, fat man with fancy clothes and a big gold chain around his neck climbed – with some difficulty – onto a bench. He looked around, cleared his throat, and started talking. I suddenly thought of the, "As mayor of Munchkin City..." song from *The Wizard of Oz,* the hit movie that had arrived from America at the end of 1939. I had to bite my lip to avoid giggling.

"Welcome to the great town of Newmarket, teachers, boys, and distinguished guests... This is the time for all good people to do their duty... um... stiff upper lip and all that... As the mayor of this fair city, and it is my honor to represent this municipality in your time of distress and great need..."

"The only distress I'm going to be feeling is if he doesn't shut up and get on with it," I whispered to Charlie.

The day had been long enough already, and one more pompous windbag was not a part of the agenda we were looking forward to at this point.

"We have over two hundred homes with families graciously willing to offer you respite and solace…"

He went on in this grandiose style, but – fortunately - for no more than three or four minutes before thankfully concluding with, "… and so I will just ask our host families to mingle and pick out their boys. Please remember to sign in on the main register before you leave, so that we will know which boys are fortunate enough to be with what families. Thank you."

I looked at Charlie with my mouth hanging open. "Did you just hear what I thought I just heard? I can't believe it. It really is going to be like one of those cattle markets we heard about!"

All over the parking lot people wandered around, looking groups of boys up and down critically. A few even made dismissive, "I don't think so," evaluations before moving on without even introducing themselves first. Some of our less enthusiastic hosts looked around doubtfully, frowned at an exceptionally grubby or tear-stained specimen, or shook their heads in disgust before moving on to greener pastures.

Most of the younger boys got snatched up almost immediately, their little cheeks pinched and their hair tousled by ladies who appeared ready to stuff the poor creatures into baby-carriages and wheel them away.

We were horrified.

"I'm beginning to feel sick," Charlie said. We edged our way to the end of the wall and sat as quiet and still as possible, trying not to be noticed.

"What if we don't get to be somewhere together?" I suddenly said. The thought had just occurred to me. "I don't think I could stand it by myself."

"Nothing much we can do about it now, is there?" Charlie replied helpfully. He looked tired and defeated.

After some time things quieted down somewhat, and we began to realize we were part of a rapidly thinning crowd.

"I don't like the looks of this." Charlie looked around anxiously. "What if we have to go home with someone mean?"

"Then we'll stand up for each other and we'll make sure it gets fixed, that's what we'll do!" I spoke with more conviction than I actually felt. What I felt was sick.

Just then, I felt a tap on my shoulder, and I turned around to be greeted by a spry middle-aged lady wearing a tattered tweed jacket, worn riding pants, and Wellington boots.

"Good afternoon, boys. My name is Lily Duncan."

"Hello. I'm Henry Bradley."

"And I'm Charlie. Charlie Green."

"Frightful scene, wouldn't you say?" Lily Duncan's eyes were dancing with a mixture of compassion and mirth.

"I haven't seen so much pushing and shoving since the last big sale at Woolworths! So I thought I'd lay low until things settled down a bit."

She scanned what was left of the crowd appraisingly.

"Then I thought I should wait around for a couple of nice young chaps who got passed over."

"Well I'd hardly say we were passed..." I stared to protest. But I could tell a genuine friend when I saw one. "Oh, never mind. We'd be delighted to accompany you. Wouldn't we, Charlie."

"Yes. Thanks. Certainly," Charlie said. "Thank you very much."

So we gathered our meager belongings together, signed out at the mayor's table, and followed Lily to an old tumbledown farm truck parked out on the side of the street. Any kind of transportation was a good sign, as many of the boys could be seen struggling down the sidewalk, school uniforms in disarray, dragging their increasingly heavy luggage as best they could.

We threw our stuff in the back of Lily's truck and hopped in. It had been a very long day.

CHAPTER TEN

It's Possible We Landed on Our Feet…

Winnie Duncan seemed sincerely delighted to have found us. "So you two boys are from Folkestone in Kent? Such a lovely town. My husband and I used to go there quite often for our holiday. The harbor area is charming. Do you ever go down to the docks?"

"Err… they won't let us anywhere near them anymore!" Charlie laughed. "But that's a long story."

"Is your husband in the army, Mrs. Duncan?" I asked.

"Goodness no. He's quite dead! But thank you for thinking I might be that young." She smiled contagiously. "Mr. Duncan passed away around ten years ago. Heart attack."

"Oh. I'm sorry," we said, together.

"Don't bother yourselves being sorry," she said kindly. "I'm sure Mr. Duncan is quite happy, and I'm sure that I am too."

She pulled the rickety truck around to the right and onto a small single lane road. Then she gunned the engine, started heading north, and consistently kept her foot on the accelerator as we headed faster and faster toward what seemed like the middle of nowhere.

"Now then boys, I must insist that you call me Lily. Mrs. Duncan is much too formal."

I peered out in to the lush fenland, not a hump or a hill in sight. The view revealed nothing but level, fertile, fields. "Where is your house, Mrs... Lily?"

"The village of Isleham. It's a little under eight miles this way on the road toward Ely. Andrew and I used to run a farm on the edge of the village. Wheat, celery, asparagus, tomatoes, a few pigs. Andrew's brother Ned does all the farming now. I still raise the pigs, have half an acre of vegetables, help Ned's wife Mary with the paperwork, and volunteer where I can."

She had the old truck up to well over fifty. We held on a little more tightly.

"Watch out for this right turn," she said, as we involuntarily leaned into the door. Amazingly, she didn't slow down one bit. "The fields were here before the roads," she explained, "so every once in a while there's a steep bend because we have to go around someone's property."

"Are many of the boys coming out to your village?" I asked.

"So far as I can tell, you're it." She smiled reassuringly. "But several of the village children do take the bus into Newmarket for school, and there's my granddaughter, Jennifer... did I mention Jennifer?"

We shook our heads.

"Oh, you'll like Jennifer." The truck sort of slowed while Lily negotiated a tight series of turns before accelerating hard into a straight, narrow road. Waves of wheat stretched for acres and acres on either side.

"Jennifer's father, my son Peter, is a Spitfire pilot in the south. He's stationed down near your way actually. She's staying here with me because her mum is doing something hush-hush with the Air Defense Command down in Dover. She's just turned sixteen."

"Sixteen!" Charlie and I both groaned and looked at each other in disgust.

"Now then boys." Lily looked playfully stern. "She's not one of those stuck up teenaged girls you're thinking of. After all, she is my granddaughter."

Well, we couldn't argue with the merits of that. Lily Duncan did seem to be an unusually nice lady. Besides, anyone who had a Spitfire pilot for a father and whose mother did "hush-hush" stuff for the government had to be fairly interesting.

A few scattered houses began to emerge from the flat landscape as we approached the village of Isleham. We drove down a wide avenue of ancient oak trees, and then turned left in front of what was obviously the central village green. We could see about ten acres of lush pasture, nicely mowed. The green was surrounded by a mixture of mature oaks and chestnuts, with a well-tended cricket pitch in the middle belying the incivility and barbarity of the war.

We turned right at the old parish church, the center of village life for hundreds of years, and were soon past the small epicenter of the community. The green, the church, and a few shops, that was it. A long straight lane then took us the last half mile to its junction with East Fen Road. We had finally arrived at the end of our long day's journey.

Lily Duncan slowed down in front of a delightful cottage, set aside from the barns and outbuildings of the farmyard next door. A neatly mown lawn curved around the front, along with some immaculate flower beds.

Our host pulled into the driveway, and around the side it was all farm. She turned the ignition key, carefully applied the handbrake, and looked around proudly. The engine sputtered a few times and seemed to sigh before finally acquiescing.

"Well, here we are then," Lily said. "Either of you boys have a penny?"

"I have the shilling I won from Mr. Thomas," Charlie offered.

"Good. Toss it."

He did.

"What does it say?"

"Heads."

"Heads it is," Lily said in her matter of fact manner. "All right then. Charles, that means you'll be staying over at Ned and Mary's place."

Charlie blanched. We both thought we were through with surprises for the day, and here was one more to deal with.

Lily laughed. "Don't worry. Before you get too excited, look across the corner of my vegetable garden."

About a hundred fifty yards away, around a high hedged lane and across multiple rows of healthy looking produce, stood an enormous old farmhouse, two barns, and a variety of interesting looking outbuildings.

"That's where Ned and Mary live." Lily put her hand on Charlie's shoulder. "You'll be coming and going like you live in both houses. But that will be your home-base for sleeping, your address, where you hang your hat, where you eat breakfast, and such like. And this will be Henry's. I don't have room for both of you, and Mary will spoil you so badly Henry will be asking to move over there too!"

Charlie looked less anxious.

"But for now, let's go inside and have a nice cup of tea. Then we'll get you all settled."

*   *   *   *

Lily's granddaughter greeted us at the door. "Well hello there, evacuees," she said. Her genuine smile and bright eyes warmed me somehow more than I had expected.

Jennifer had long, dark brown hair that hung in waves alongside an oval face alive with expression. Her hazel eyes shone brightly under a high forehead, and her enthusiastic welcome was accentuated by the brilliance of her smile. I had not intended to pay such close attention, but I could not help but notice her toned, balanced, athletic physique.

Simply put, Jennifer was stunningly beautiful. She gave her grandmother a quick hug, and kissed her lightly on the cheek. "Missed you, Granny."

The door opened into a large kitchen, a room that had been combined with the living space to form what Lily called, "a cozy country kitchen." The floor was all brick with a variety of rugs defining different parts of the room. We walked past the large coal-burning stove, dropping our luggage alongside a long, inviting sofa. In front of the sofa sat a low, wide coffee table, covered to a significant depth with current newspapers, a pile of well-thumbed magazines, and several thick books.

Opposite the sofa, which effectively cut off that part of the room from the kitchen, an enormous fireplace took up most of the space. On the same wall as the outside door there was a bulging bay window, complete with cushioned window seat. A few more books littered the seat and, opposite that, alongside the door that led to the rest of the house, was a floor to ceiling set of built in bookshelves that overflowed with inviting titles. This I would have to investigate later, at leisure.

I felt a touch on my arm. Jennifer was standing beside me with a gleam in her eye. "What are you standing there rubbing your hands together so greedily about?" she laughed.

"Books," was all I said. "Books, and more books."

"Then you've come to the right place," she smiled.

Charlie was in the kitchen, helping Lily with a tray of goodies, making himself at home. "Tea time!" he yelled, like he'd been living in Lily's kitchen all his life.

"Put those things on the coffee table, Charles," Lily instructed. "I'll bring the pot."

We instinctively sat down, as our newfound friend hovered over the cups and saucers.

"Here you go, Henry."

"Thanks." The tea was perfect. It was as if she already knew I liked just a little sugar – a luxury in wartime. I watched carefully as she did the same for Charlie.

"Thank you, Mrs. Duncan," Charlie said.

"That's 'Lily,' Charles. You really must call me Lily."

"Oh. Yes. Sorry." My friend was having a hard time articulating with his mouth stuffed full of buttered scone.

"Making our own butter here on the farm is a big help," Lily explained as my eyes almost bugged out of my head. Rationing was very strict throughout England, especially in the towns. I had not seen that much butter on a single piece of bread in a very long time.

Jennifer emerged from the kitchen with a large, steaming mug.

"Jennifer. Must you, dear?"

"What? The unseemly mug – or the coffee?" She smiled at her grandmother over the top of her drink. "Come on, Granny, you know that I can't stand tea."

"I know that you can't stand convention," Lily retorted. "I suspect that you don't have a problem with tea."

Jennifer sighed, smiled, shrugged her shoulders, and squeezed her grandmother's hand.

"Just don't dunk your biscuit. I will most certainly draw the line at dunking." Mrs. Duncan feigned disgust and sipped daintily from her china cup.

Suddenly Jennifer sprang up, disappeared, and then reemerged excitedly carrying a carefully folded piece of paper.

"I got a great letter from Dad today. Do you want to hear? You don't mind, do you?" she said, looking at Charlie and me apologetically.

I smiled my assent, Lily nodded, and Jennifer began. I felt myself settling comfortably into my chair, an unexpected sense of ease creeping over me. Sharing this news from her dad was as natural for Jennifer as welcoming us into the house, or making tea for, "the evacuees."

I felt something extremely natural and comforting in the welcoming atmosphere of this small family. Lily and Jennifer projected an authentic sense of belonging and wellbeing that I really didn't experience all that much back in my own home.

"I dunno," I said to Charlie, later, "I think this situation is going to turn out all right after all."

CHAPTER ELEVEN

Settling in and Looking Around

My room was the kind of space that would qualify for the designation, "quaint" if it had been written up in a tour guide. The compact space was obviously one of those afterthought adaptations back when the cottage had originally been constructed. "Let's see," the builder must have said, "what can we cram into this tiny alcove?"

Maybe it had first been designed as a sewing room, or a home office, or a study – maybe even a large closet? I wasn't sure. But it was sleeping quarters now. I could tell because somehow a single bed had been squeezed in, leveraged under the ample window.

The bed accounted for just about the extent of the furnishings. I paced the room off, six feet wide by nine and a half feet long. Eighteen inches of the width was taken up by built-in cupboards and shelves. At the end of the bed, an abbreviated desk had been hand crafter to fit the snug alcove. The wooden floor was covered by a rich but well-worn oriental rug. Everything was spotless.

Whitewashed walls, white painted shelves, no dust on the floor, and all sixteen individual window panes were crystal clear.

Through the window I could see a small brick patio, several well-tended flower beds, a wooden bench, two colorful bird-feeders, and a wrought-iron gate connecting to a footpath through the rows of vegetables beyond.

"It's all yours," Lily said, warmly. "Arrange the room however you want – not that there's any other way you could fit the furniture!" She laughed.

"This was our farm office in the old days, before Ned took over the business end. I'm very pleased that the bed fit – if only just!"

Then Lily looked at me a little sternly and cleared her throat. "There's something you need to know." She stiffened just a little, as if to emphasize the importance of what she was going to say. "I'm very strict when it comes to cleanliness."

She must have seen my downcast expression.

"Now don't be disheartened, dear, there is a balance here...." She could tell how nervous I was feeling. "... because I have no agenda at all regarding tidy."

I felt myself involuntarily wipe my hand slowly across my forehead.

"Do you understand, Henry?" she asked. "I don't mean to sound harsh – but cleanliness is one of my things."

"Not a problem," I said. "I think I've got it. Clean is important. But, so long as things are clean, then it's okay if my room isn't really all that neat."

"Well done, Henry. That's exactly correct."

To be honest, I was actually quite relieved. This was excellent, and also quite the turnabout for me. Back home in Folkestone, everything was pretty much the exact opposite. My dad would often storm unannounced into my room to rant and rave about how it looked. "Get this place straight and make up that bed, Henry. When I walk into a room I want to see it tidy. Got it? Tidy."

I surmised that my room could have been filthy. Dirty sheets and smelly socks were apparently no problem to Dr. Doom, just so long as they looked lined up and orderly. Just smooth things over on the surface, and he didn't care what it was really like underneath.

Charlie stuck his head in my room. "Hey, Henry, throw your stuff on your bed and we can go over and check out my place. Mrs. Duncan says it's time. You can unpack later."

My friend looked around appraisingly. "Nice closet... room... whatever. Just as well you don't have much stuff to unpack! Come on. Let's go."

Charlie already had his leather satchel hanging on his shoulder, and his overstuffed duffle bag in his hand. Then, probably because it felt like we were still on some kind of a school fieldtrip, he pulled his school cap out of his pocket and fitted it snugly on his head.

"Come along with me, boys. I have to see to it that you're properly introduced." Lily started out of the door and down the road toward the neighbors.

She had a natural brisk walking pace, similar to the one my mother sported when she had more shopping than time. It wasn't that she appeared in a hurry, or impatient, or pushy, she was just focused one hundred percent on the next thing on her list. Therefore, walking from point A to point B must be accomplished as efficiently as possible.

Lily was a good ten yards ahead of Charlie and me by the time she reached the end of her driveway. She turned around to hurry us, but then remembered this was our first time out on the farm, and it had been a very long day. She paused to allow us to catch up. I could tell it was a real effort for here to walk at a leisurely speed.

The sky glowed with England's signature June luminescence, the kind of eternally lit burn that smolders late into the evening as Britain's high latitudes approach the summer solstice, leaving the countryside illuminated as if from the inside. I almost instantly loved the place.

"Why is the road built up so much higher than the fields?" Charlie wanted to know. "I noticed that on the drive over too." He always enjoyed learning the small details, wanting to know the interesting facts that most of us casually overlook.

"We call this part of England *The Fen Country*, Charles," Lily answered. "We're pretty close to sea-level, and everything is so low here the fields quickly get saturated when it's wet. If the roads weren't built up like small causeways, then they'd turn into virtual rivers every time it rains. If that happened then we'd all be stuck!"

"Hmm," Charlie nodded his head. "Interesting."

"When we go over to Ely to visit the cathedral one day, you'll see that the whole city sits on slightly higher ground," Lily explained. "It's called *The Isle of Ely* because it stands up from the marshlands. The city really was almost a proper island before the fens were drained. At one time - centuries in the past - all this farmland was either marsh or part of the North Sea. That's why it is all so fertile today, and one of the many reasons we grow the best crops in all of England."

The road looped around Lily's extensive vegetable garden before approaching the front of a large rambling farmyard. Three enthusiastic dogs came running down to the gate, barking mildly and wagging their tails furiously.

"My guess is these are not exactly ferocious guard dogs!" I laughed.

"Boys, meet Gyp, Blackie, and Newton."

We were pounced, licked, circled, and sniffed accordingly. Having exchanged the obligatory greetings, our three new friends took off around the outbuildings to fulfill some other pressing social engagement.

Lily smiled, and then herded us toward the farmhouse. "Come on up and meet Charles's hosts."

We were greeted at the door by a friendly middle-aged woman in an obviously well-used apron. She was wiping evidence of some recent cooking from her hands. We were invited into the kitchen, where a dark, thunderous looking man was drinking tea and eating an enormous slab of bread and cheese.

"Ned, this 'ere is te new boy, young Charles." Mary smiled enthusiastically in the general direction of Charlie by way of encouragement. "E's just 'ere from down Folkestone way."

"O aye." Ned gave a halfway nod, never even glancing up from his plate of food.

Charlie looked nervously at Lily. She laughed. "It's all right, Charles," she said. "Ned's not much of one for talking."

"Aye," continued Mary, "te men folks up roond this way don't go much for words."

Ned got up and washed his hands at the kitchen sink. He strode to the back door, stopped, looked at Charlie appraisingly, nodded, and said, "I reckon thou'lt do, lad." Then he was gone.

We watched Ned make his way through the yard. He drove off on a tractor, pipe sticking sideways from his mouth. Several barn cats lounged lazily at the entrance to one of the buildings, unaffected by the noise of the sputtering machine.

Mary watched her husband through the window.

"E won't be back afore dark," mused Mary. "Not now while te weather's fair and te evenings long. There's much that needs be doing, and te young men folk off at war."

Mary shook her head, sadly. "You boys may be a mite help come around 'arvest." The thought seemed to brighten her. "Now 'ow 'bout some tea, then?"

"No, thank you," Charlie replied. "We just had a whole boatload over at Lily's."

"We'll leave Charles to get settled." Lily motioned me toward the door. "I know you boys are tired, and we'll make an early night of it. The word is: 'no school tomorrow.' Everyone gets another full day to rest up and get nicely settled in."

"Most excellent," I observed. "See you in the morning, Charlie."

"Not too early," he grinned.

*   *   *   *

Back at Lily's house I made my way to my new room to unpack, and see what I could do to personalize the space.

"Beans on toast for supper, Henry," Lily yelled down the hall. "About thirty minutes." I could tell right away there would always be good food and plenty around here.

"Jennifer dear, please set the table when you're done with those flowers."

"Yes, Granny."

There wasn't much in my suitcase for me to put away. I found the right drawers for shirts, socks, underwear, and pants. I found a place in the bathroom for my toothbrush. And my school things fit neatly in and around the tiny desk.

Additionally, I had squeezed in three of my favorite books, trying my best to find room in my travel bag. But now – with the extensive and inviting home library in Lily's living room – I regretted having wasted the space to pack them.

Nonetheless, J.R.R Tolkien's *The Hobbit*, a treasured edition of *The Complete Sherlock Holmes*, and an extensive collection of stories by Kipling graced a small section of the built-in shelves. They had the effect of helping me feel at least a little as if this was ow my own private space.

Finally, I rummaged around in the bottom of my suitcase for the last few personal items. I was glad my tablet of sketching paper was not bent. Then there were twelve good quality drawing pencils held together by a rubber band, my pocket knife – a real "Buck," sent by some second cousin in the United States, and – lastly – a small framed picture of my family, taken on holiday in Cornwall the previous summer.

I placed the picture carefully on the shelf, angled carefully so that my father was mostly hidden behind the adjacent book. My mother and I, at least, smiled out on the room, looking for the most part like a contented family.

"It's almost time for supper," called Jennifer. She leaned her head into my room, bright eyes framed by the mass of dark, wavy hair that fell to her shoulders. "All unpacked now?"

"Well until the lorries come with the rest of my stuff!" I laughed. "But seriously, I've pulled out every one of the few things I had room for."

I smiled ruefully. "It's hard to believe that I can unload all my stuff and a room this small still manages to look empty."

Jennifer stepped inside the door frame and stretched, arching her back, reaching both arms in a massive "Y" as high as she could go, all five fingers of each hand splayed open. She leaned against the wall and offered a conspiratorial smile.

"There's a war on, you know." She chuckled at her use of the already well-worn cliché. "And besides, we share everything in Granny's house. So it turns out that you have a lot more than you think."

*   *   *   *

Jennifer was right; I had so much and it just about overwhelmed me. I'm not usually all that emotional, and I really didn't want to find myself crying at both ends of this long day. But in that moment it was all I could do not to let the tears that suddenly filled my eyes spill over. So I squeezed my eyelids tight, pretended I needed to blow my nose, and held on.

This had, after all, been a very intense day. It started at home, with goodbyes, and strain, and not knowing; it became filled up with both tension and relief as we realized we were not ending up in a dismal location; and it was ending, now, with the generous and open-spirited kindness of total strangers, strangers who were already, and without a second thought, trusted friends.

I was determined to take a deep breath, count my blessings, and do the stiff upper lip thing regardless. I was almost sixteen years old, the German army was poised to cross the English Channel, life was in the balance, and I had a new – ready-made - family. I really had to get a grip.

CHAPTER TWELVE

"We Shall Fight on the Beaches"

Charlie and I landed on our feet in a big way for a couple of refugee evacuees. We had boarded the train in Folkestone at the whim of chance - or, if we were lucky, mercy. In the end we were blessed by providence and kindness with a much better state of affairs than either one of us could have hoped or imagined. The contrast between our situation, and the awful evacuation scenarios we had dreamed up in our worst fears, was not lost on me.

Of course it was "early days" yet, but I already felt confident Charlie and I were well situated to make the very best of what was an undeniably difficult situation for the entire nation.

We were obviously part of a positive atmosphere, plugged in with two friendly families who were more than happy to give us a home. Then there was the location. *The Fens* of Cambridgeshire were going to be a great place to spend the summer, or however long it was going to take for England to work out what to do about Mr. Hitler and his absurd desire to rule the world.

After breakfast Monday morning Charlie and I devoted the best part of an hour to a detailed Ordnance Survey chart of the immediate area. We opened the map on the living room floor and huddled over it, plotting out our new home.

Isleham is a small village in a region of small villages. The quiet country lanes, the fields, the streams, the stories, the history, and the interesting destinations suggested wonderful possibilities for walking, biking, and exploring. Even the larger communities like Newmarket and Ely were accessible if we had a whole day, and if we could find some bikes available to ride.

"Check out all this area here," Jennifer said, leaning over the map and running her hand across an enormous swath of land. "This is all farmland, it's hundreds of acres. It all used to be worked by Grandma Lily and Grandpa Andrew back in the day. Now Gran leases out just about all of the fields for other people to manage. She still owns most of the spread, as Grandpa Andrew made her promise to never let the land leave the family."

"I wouldn't have guessed she was that rich?" I said.

"Rich? I don't think so! You only say that because most people have no idea that land and wealth don't necessarily add up to the same thing!" Jennifer laughed and shook her head.

"After taxes and upkeep, each acre has to produce a certain amount of income, or else it simply costs more money to own than the land is really worth. That's why Gran is leasing so much of it out. Unless you can work it yourself, then all that acreage is nothing more than a big headache. Agricultural land that's not busy is like feeding a house full of relatives who don't have jobs and don't pay rent."

"Does that mean your dad's going to move out here and farm the land when he's through flying Spitfires?" Charlie asked.

"I really wish he would," Jennifer said, wistfully. "Only I think he's turned into more of a big city guy. But wouldn't it be marvelous to live out here in a big house and know that all the land around belonged to you?"

"So where did you live before the war?" I asked.

"London. Dad has a law practice and mum used to write stories for women's magazines."

"Your mother's a writer?"

"I guess so. But it's not exactly what the critics tend to call serious literature. I love my mum, and I'm glad she enjoys writing, but personally I'm not into that kind of story."

"What kind of story is that?" I asked.

"You know, 'Romance,'" Jennifer made a face. "Mum writes the kind of fluff where some famous pirate kidnaps the wife of some evil count, and then they fall in love. Of course it turns out that the pirate is really a good guy caught in a bad situation, and the real villain is the evil count what's his name. After a couple of big swashbuckling scenes, lots of dancing, more fights, plus tons of unnecessary kissing, everything works out for true love. The end. Blah, blah, blah, blah."

Charlie and I grimaced. Not our kind of story either.

"Do you live in the center of London?"

"Yes. We have an enormous townhouse near Hyde Park."

"Do you miss it?"

"Once in a while," Jennifer said. "Living in the city can be loads of fun, but then sometimes I'm just glad to be away from all the noise, out here where things are so peaceful." She looked down at the map again.

"I know what I'll do," she continued. "I'll become a famous actress, so I can keep a house in London too. I'll stay in town – 'town' is what real Londoners call the city – when the countryside gets too boring."

Jennifer threw an imaginary boa around her neck, puffed at an imaginary cigarette, and smiled grandly for the cameras. To be honest, it was no stretch of the imagination at all to visualize her in such a glamorous role.

     *   *   *   *

It turns out the village of Isleham is slap bang in the middle of some of the best farm country in all England. There are wide open spaces all around, and that's what was needed, along with the rich fertile soil, to make a farm work.

That first full day Charlie and I must have walked close to ten miles in and around the village. Exploring was in our blood, and we wanted to know the community as thoroughly as we could and as quickly as possible. It turned out that just about everyone who lived there was involved in agriculture on some level, and there were yards stacked full with farm equipment on almost every street.

Local farming had become even more important now that the government wanted to avoid importing so much food from overseas. Every day Merchant Marine convoys from the other side of the Atlantic were forced to run the blockade of German U-Boats. Many of the vessels did not make it. So anything the provincial communities could do to produce food locally was a massive contribution to the ongoing war effort.

In 1940 there were around thirty-eight million people living in England, all jammed onto a mere fifty thousand square miles of land. It's an area a little smaller than the American state of Louisiana. Consequently, every cleared acre of fertile ground was chock full of vegetables and grains. People were raising food in their own back gardens, too – a project the government encouraged, resourced, and dubbed, "Victory Gardens."

Listening to the locals talk about how it all worked, Charlie and I learned that the folk who actually produce the food are impacted less by rationing than the city dwellers who depend on the local grocery store for most of their produce. Meat was always going to be an issue, but most of everything else was in bountiful supply out in the country, right there in the middle of the farms.

When it came to food, it looked like we were certainly fortunate to be in the right place at the right time.

The village of Isleham may have been very small, but it still had pretty much everything we needed. There was a general store, a post office, a news agents, a fish and chip shop that the news agent opened in the evenings (depending on supply), a couple of churches, and the beautiful village green. The farms and fields that surrounded the community were fascinating, and all the people we met were – without exception – genuinely pleased to have us as visitors in their village.

We almost felt like celebrities. Or – as Jennifer pointed out – "our pet evacuees." Charlie and I both said we wished Graham could be there to share the experience with us.

*   *   *   *

At the end of that first full day, Lily summoned Charlie and me to the kitchen. She was in the middle of making the ever-present pot of tea, and made us sit down at the table.

"How long have you been here?" she demanded. She wore a stern look on her face.

"Almost twenty-four hours," I replied, nervously, wondering what we could possibly have done to get ourselves into trouble this quickly.

"And exactly how many letters have you written home to your parents?" she asked, glowering at me and Charlie over her glasses and looking impressively fierce.

"I'm asking because the post has already gone over to Newmarket for the London train," she said. "And I didn't see it bulging with letters addressed to Folkestone. Well?"

Charlie and I looked at each other sheepishly.

"Consider this," Lily reminded us. "Yesterday morning your poor parents put you on a train with no idea of where you were headed. When you boarded that train, the evacuation of Dunkirk was not quite complete, and so far as I know it still may not be. At this point we don't know what the German army is going to do from day to day."

She paused for a moment to let all that sink in.

"There is a good chance," she continued, "that our country will be invaded by Nazis. Who knows, maybe they'll land on the beaches in the next twenty-four hours! And such an invasion remains an imminent possibility every twenty-four hours after that, and the day after that, until all the king's horses and all the king's men can come up with some way to make them go away!"

I have to admit she was stating a very strong case!

"So, don't you boys think that now would be a good time to at least let your mother and father know where to find you, just in case their whole world falls to pieces and they still don't even know your address!"

I don't know about Charlie, but I suddenly felt terrible. Fortunately, Lily had both a cup of tea and plentiful writing supplies handy. I honestly don't think she would have let us leave the table without two carefully written, sealed, addressed, and stamped letters.

> June 3rd, 1940
> Dear Mum:
> Yesterday's train ride was quite an experience.
> Eventually, after changing in London and getting
> bused over to Liverpool Street, we took the train to
> Cambridge, and then on to Newmarket (you know,
> the place with the race horses). It was a zoo out
> there, with people grabbing kids like they were sale
> items at Woolworth's. Charlie and I kept an extra
> low profile till Mrs. Lily Duncan searched us out
> and rescued us from a life of certain misery!
> Lily drove us here to the village of Isleham,
> where Charlie and I get to be neighbors. We are the
> only Folkestone kids not living in Newmarket. Don't
> worry about that, though, because we already like it
> here and we will be going into town for school every
> day. Lily has a smashing granddaughter, Jennifer,
> the village is full of farms, and we are happy with
> where we ended up.
> School starts tomorrow. We will be taking the
> bus in with the other village kids. Apparently, we
> leave here at seven o'clock, but school will be over
> for the day by noon (we will be sharing the school.
> Folkestone kids go to class in the mornings, and then
> the Newmarket kids all afternoon).
> I miss you very much, and we're worried about
> what will happen in Folkestone if the Germans try to
> come over. At the moment, this still feels like a

holiday, but I am sure that will change when school
gets going in the morning.
  I love you, mum.
  - Henry

c/o Mrs. Lily Duncan
Duncan Farms, East Fen Road
Isleham, Cambridgeshire

"That's much better," Lily said when we had both finished our
letters, addressed the envelopes, and attached the stamps that she
had provided. "Now, run up the street to the post office and drop
them in the main box before you do anything else."

"Yes, Mrs. Duncan... Lily. Thanks," we said in unison.

"And boys," she fixed us with a very directive gaze, "there will
be one more letter the day after tomorrow, and yet another one
before the week is out. Do you understand?"

"Absolutely," we smiled. Lily may be a sweet natured lady, but
when she meant business, we had the distinct impression that there
really were not any options other than one-hundred percent
compliance. We hurried up the street to mail our letters.

*   *   *   *

Newmarket was only eight miles away. It was also the nearest
market-sized town, the go-to destination for more serious
shopping, and the place where a lot of important business got
transacted. Most importantly, Newmarket was where Charlie and I
would be going to school.

Lessons started much too early in the morning for our liking,
but at least it got the academic day over with. Two fair-sized

schools were now sharing the one building, so the simplest solution was to run one early shift, then an afternoon session for the out of town visitors.

Unlike the rest of our Folkestone buddies, Charlie and I ended up attending morning school with the locals. The bus was not about to make an extra trip out to our village just for the two of us.

At first we were disappointed, and school officials started to talk about reassigning us to lodging in the town. But we quickly reevaluated the situation, and realized how much we enjoyed our housing arrangements, living on the farm with Lily. So we decided we'd much rather do our best to make things work. Thankfully, everyone else agreed. Charlie and I got to stay in Isleham and stick with the plan.

Some bright spark even came up with the suggestion that we might want to ride bicycles all the way from Isleham and back every day, just so we could attend classes with our Folkestone teachers. But the school was located on the far side of Newmarket, over ten miles from the farm.

"We like you and all that," we told Mr. Thomas when he took us aside to talk about it, "but we don't like you enough for more than twenty miles of pedaling every day!"

Eventually we grew to appreciate the schedule, and also the status we achieved with the kids from the local community. Not only did we enjoy being out of class by noon, and away from the school once lunch was done, but people felt like they were contributing to the war effort by being as nice to us as possible.

The Newmarket community was a decent place to be, with friendly teachers. We also found out that not having a "checkered history" (or a "reputation") to live down restored the all-important, benefit of the doubt we'd long since lost with our regular school staff, due to getting ourselves into trouble so much - even (mostly) fairly innocent trouble, before we were evacuated from Folkestone.

After that first day of school, Tuesday June 4th, Charlie and I sat around the kitchen table for afternoon tea with Lily and Jennifer. We were excited, noisily sharing all the details, while Jennifer complained loudly that "the evacuees" had ruined her schedule, and that no one should be forced to get on a bus quite so early every morning!

Suddenly, Lily got out of her seat and turned up the volume on the radio. She set it to "high," and she put her finger to her lips with a look of urgency.

"Listen!" she instructed. "The evacuation of Dunkirk is finally complete. They say it has been a splendid success. Now they're going to play some of the Prime Minister's speech."

It was a surreal sensation, huddled around an old radio, listening to Winston Churchill talk so plainly about the dire predicament we were in as a nation, pointing to the abject danger vested in every single moment. The Prime Minister's words were words I needed to hear, and they remain words I will never ever forget. The speech chilled me and it encouraged me too. I was scared and fired up, all at the same time:

"We shall go on to the end," the Prime Minister assured us, *"We shall fight in France; we shall fight on the seas and oceans; we shall fight with growing confidence and growing strength in the air; we shall defend our island, whatever the cost may be; we shall fight on the beaches; we shall fight on the landing grounds; we shall fight in the fields and in the streets; we shall fight in the hills; we shall never surrender...."*

It was magnificent, and it was frightening. Winston Churchill literally expected the Nazi invasion to happen possibly the very next hour, or the very next day, maybe within a week. And if not now, the possibility loomed every following day – one relentless dawn after another – until Hitler's army could finally be driven back.

Churchill wanted us to be prepared.

I remember holding hands – I don't know how that happened. It was just the four of us, sitting quietly and listening. Then a lot of silence. Silence, holding hands, and not talking.

Not talking at all. Just taking it all in.

C HAPTER THIRTEEN

Weeding Ned's Celery and Driving the Tractor

We soon realized why the local schools had been so willing to choose the morning shift. In the war economy there was a mountain of agricultural work to be done. With most of the local young men already signed up to join the army, an enormous labor gap was left on the farms, just at the time when food production was most critical. Early morning school freed up long afternoons for kids to help in the fields.

Our hosts were kind enough to make it clear that Charlie and I were not expected to participate. But we volunteered nonetheless, putting in a lot of long, warm, days out in the June sun.

Charlie took more naturally to the work than I did. In fact, he bonded almost immediately with the whole farming way of life. It was as if he had been waiting for such an opportunity to come along.

I asked him about it after we had only been in Isleham for about a week. He had offered to go out with Ned every single afternoon, sometimes staying in the fields until after dark, putting schoolwork off – quite literally – until the cows came home.

"You know the vegetable patch I enjoy planting in our back garden in Folkestone?" Charlie said. He had been the victim of a lot of ribbing from me and Graham ever since he was about six years old, the same time he started his own flower and vegetable garden behind the house with his dad.

"Well, yes. I still can't believe you like pottering around back there like an old man, when there is so much fun to be had doing just about anything else?"

"Garden art is wasted on the crude tastes of the uncultivated," he retorted. "Anyway, I may not have told you this, but I've always wanted to be a farmer."

"Get out!"

"Seriously," Charlie smiled. "The idea of acres of wheat, rows of vegetables, bales of straw, the smell of fresh cut hay... I love it. I'm not so sure about messing around with livestock, but growing stuff is amazing!"

That afternoon we both hiked out to one of Ned's celery fields with Frank, an older gentleman who had been working with the family for about a hundred years. Frank was essentially a point and grunt communicator, and it took us a while to get a clear set of guidelines for the job we'd signed up to do.

Like asparagus, celery in this part of England is a winter vegetable, and the crop was not going to be harvested for many months. However, and just like painting a house, preparation is a good three-quarters of the work. In the vegetable's early days (it had been planted around the middle of May), our job was to keep the emerging plants clear of opportunistic weeds.

We each carried a hoe – a four foot long pole with a flat-bladed cutting tool on the end – and we were supposed to work with a short chopping motion alongside each celery plant, one stalk at a time. We had to bend slightly with each down stroke, and before long I was complaining about my aching lower back. Frank, who we noticed walked around with a permanent stoop, laughed at us and then went back to grunting more vague weeding instructions in our general direction.

The first hour was horrible. I must have destroyed at least twenty-five percent of the celery in my row! The sun was beating down like we were in the Sahara Desert, and nothing about the afternoon felt anything like the middle of June in England - at least not to me. With each row exactly a quarter mile long, we were not supposed to straighten up and stretch until a given line of celery was done.

It took the entire first sixty minutes to complete just the one row. When I looked around, Charlie was halfway down his third. He had taken to celery wedding like a duck to water.

"What is your problem, overachiever?" I yelled, hardly able to stand straight up enough to see him.

"No problem at all," Charlie replied. "Isn't this fun?"

My friend walked over to where I was still gasping for breath. "Here, have some water. I must admit," he continued, "that it did take a few minutes to find my rhythm. Don't tell Frank," he whispered quietly, "but I accidentally whacked a couple of actual celery plants before I perfected my technique."

"You feel guilty about a couple of dead plants!" I choked. "You found your rhythm?" I gasped. "And then you perfected your technique," I sputtered. "Good grief, Charlie, there must be close to a hundred decapitated future celery failures out there in my row. I still haven't found any rhythm, and I can't imagine doing even another twenty minutes of this miserable work!"

It did get a little easier, and I was able to finish out the afternoon without causing too much extra damage to the crop. But the experience taught me to be a little more selective with my volunteering. After a long bath, back at Lily's cottage, I fooled myself into believing I was feeling better. But the next morning's bumpy bus ride in to school just about killed my lower back. Meanwhile, Charlie sat comfortable and happy, as if he had been happily hoeing rows of winter celery all his life.

*   *   *   *

The antique tractor was another issue entirely. I had been anxious to drive something mechanical for years. There always seemed to be material that needed to be hauled from one field to another. Other times, there was no end of endless circling around a series of acres or two to pick up straw, or hay, or simply move some piece of heavy equipment.

A lot of farmers still used horses, but Lily and Andrew had farmed on a larger scale, harvesting and then marketing with more commercial success than most landowners.

Consequently, *Duncan Farms* boasted more mechanization than the standard rural operation. Fuel was scarce, yes, but Ned managed what resources they had carefully, and his production numbers justified the small petrol pump parked outside the big equipment barn.

Ned, in typical fashion, sat me on the seat and proceeded to offer the absolute minimum in terms of instruction.

"Thou'lt find te lever 'ere'll work te gears."

What was that again?

"Mind te clutch; she's an 'ard en."
So, what exactly is a clutch?
"This 'ere brake'll do."

Then he disappeared through the hedgerow, along with Charlie. As if by now – and because of his instructions - I knew everything there was to know about driving a tractor! Ned suggested I follow them to the next field when I felt comfortable enough with my driving.

Well I sat there, perched on the hard metal seat atop what amounted to an enormous engine equipped with two huge wheels to hold it up, and then two smaller ones for steering.

I pushed the appropriate button and the engine sputtered to life. Then I glanced around nervously, glad to be in the middle of a recently harvested hayfield as well as at least a quarter mile from any hedgerow, in all four directions. The brake turned out to be a long handle, sitting at a thirty degree angle just below my left hand. I pulled it up a little, felt it release against the spring, and let the lever slip to the floor.

Next, I needed to figure out how to move the gears. I started to work the handle thing Ned had indicated, but then quickly stopped when a horrible grinding noise reminded me how important it was to disengage the clutch first. I rapidly came to the understanding that this was not going to be as easy as I had imagined. But it had to be better than permanently bending down to chop at miles and miles of new celery.

Eventually, I found what must have been the clutch. Then I wiggled the gear lever and turned my attention to the gas. Next I did all three things simultaneously, and – it turns out - far too fast. That was a big mistake. When the gear bit, the tractor stuttered forward maybe a couple of feet, and – essentially at the exact same time – the engine stalled. I came close to falling off the seat.

Pulling up the brake, I disengaged the gear with another loud crunch. Beads of sweat broke out all over my forehead. I was determined to make this work.

Okay, I thought. I should do just one thing at a time. So I started the engine, slowly depressed the clutch, and then worked the gear lever into what I thought must be the initial selection. Next, holding my breath, I ever so slowly let the clutch back up, feeling carefully for the moment where I could detect the pull of the engine on the gears, as the transmission started to work on the tractor's wheels. I felt something straining, and confidently let the clutch come farther back. Nothing happened. So I applied more weight on the gas pedal. I could feel the tires trying their best to turn, but there was a scraping noise that increased in direct proportion to the intensification of the amount of gas.

"Damn it…"

Suddenly I remembered I must have forgotten to disengage the brake. Not thinking about the fact that I had been unconsciously but determinedly adding potential power by pushing down on the accelerator, I reached my hand down and released the brake.

The tractor abruptly lurched forward, and I was thrown back into my seat with unexpected violence and impressive torque. I was almost jettisoned from the tractor, and hung on for dear life as the vehicle surged with a rush of initial speed. I was moving faster than I thought possible in a battered farmyard work vehicle dating from the early nineteen thirties!

Immediately, leaning heavily on several years of boy scouting and other specialized training, I panicked.

My celebrated one-quarter mile safety zone evaporated rapidly, the distance closing all the more speedily because the runaway tractor was piloted by a city boy too petrified to think clearly, too scared to realize the round thing in my hands was a steering wheel capable of saving my life, and too terrified to comprehend that the throbbing rectangle of steel beneath my foot was accelerating in direct proportion to the pressure placed upon it.

The hedgerow ahead loomed with growing menace. And still I sat, transfixed, as the intervening gap closed with mathematical inevitability.

Suddenly, fate played a hand and I hit a deep furrow in the grass, hard enough to lose my balance. I pulled on the steering wheel to right myself and was amazed to discover a slight change in direction. Thus encouraged, I pulled at the wheel again, eventually transcribing a curve that steered the tractor clear of approaching doom with less than twenty feet to spare. At the same time I pulled my foot back from the gas pedal, and was delighted to note an immediate reduction in speed.

Encouraged, I played with the gas pedal, off and on, fluctuating velocity as I went round and round in an extended circle. Then I selected a forward motion equivalent to walking speed, and steered my way in a careful pattern around the field until I felt comfortable with my control and sense of direction.

Lastly, I made my way back to the middle and stopped, turning off the engine and returning everything to its initial status quo.

I took a couple of deep breaths, went through a mental checklist, and started over, triumphantly getting the tractor moving, safely, without any hitches. I stopped, started, and stopped again. I even managed a creditable figure eight.

Eventually I felt sure that the tractor was prepared and ready to go anywhere I wanted, and when I wanted. Then, confidently, I started the engine once more and made my way into the adjacent field.

Ned had a trailer waiting, full of newly bundled bales of hay.

CHAPTER FOURTEEN

Reading Letters from Home

My first letter from home bought up a smorgasbord of sentiments. It was newsy, tender, worrisome, direct, and guilt-producing. The letter made me happy, it made me cry, and it made me angry. I didn't want to be angry, but I couldn't help myself.

> Mrs. Charles T. Bradley
> 12 Avers Road
> Folkestone, Kent
> June 12th, 1940
>
> Dear Henry,
> Thank you for writing so promptly. If felt so strange to send you off like that and not have any idea of where you were going. I'm so glad you're with such a lovely person as Mrs. Duncan. Isleham sounds like a nice village.

Just think, I heard that some children have been sent all the way to the North of England, Wales, and even Scotland!

I saw Graham Fern's mother out at the shops yesterday. I think he's already a little lonely. Why don't you write him a nice letter? Do you see much of your friend Charles? Oh, of course, you already mentioned that he is staying next door.

Just the day after you boys went away a German shell came over from France and hit the big laundry down near the seafront. It doesn't seem at all right, does it? Folkestone is such a lovely seaside town, and I just can't understand why anyone would do a thing like that.

Reverend Carlyle prayed especially for all you young people in church this Sunday – I never did see such an empty children's Sunday-school section. Don't forget to go to church, dear. Will you have to go by yourself, or does the Duncan family attend?

Henry, I think that you hurt your father's feelings by not mentioning him in your letter. Please try to think well of him. I believe you know he only does what he thinks is best.

Well I must go to the shops now. Please give Mrs. Duncan my best. Write soon.

Much love, and lots of hugs. Mum

Well, I wasn't about to start writing letters to my dad! If I had been thinking about him, then I would have written something. Maybe, "Dear Mum and Dad." But, honestly, Dr. Doom hadn't even entered my mind. So too bad about him.

The Duncan family was so completely different! There was such warmth and spontaneity between Lily and Jennifer that it felt as if they were best friends as well as relatives. And Jennifer talked all the time. She talked so openly and so lovingly about her mum and dad. Then here I was - a stranger Lily picked up in a train station parking lot - and they included me easily in all the conversation and the intimacy, without question.

Charlie, too, just like he was another brother.

Back at our house in Folkestone, it always felt like Charlie and Graham were considered inconvenient intrusions when they came over to my place. "Use the service entrance, please." As for staying for meals, something like that almost never happened, and certainly then by appointment only. It was like an unspoken but clearly understood line of demarcation: "You're welcome to play with Henry, but don't bother us."

To be honest, my friends were strangers around my family, never really allowed to be a part of it. But not here. Here Lily talked with me and Charlie like we were real people. We were both integrated into the vital fabric of family life, without reservation. Charlie could chat in the kitchen with Lily, smell something good cooking, and ask if he could stay to eat. I don't think Charlie had done much more than walk through our kitchen on his way through the house back in Folkestone.

That's when Jennifer underlined exactly what I was feeling by spontaneously sharing the latest communication from her parents.

"Listen! Listen to this, everybody. It's from my dad." Jennifer bounced around, flourishing her letter over the bread and jam as if this was the most exciting event in her life.

"Are you listening? I'll skip the first boring part... then it picks up here..."

> "... I'll bet you're not having as much fun there
> as we are down here in Kent. After an exciting

afternoon shooting down Jerry (German planes)
over the Channel, a car load of us drove over to
Dover to see your mum. Boy, was she ever
surprised! We stayed up well after midnight
talking. We laughed out loud about last year's
family trip to Exmouth. Remember?

Of course we talked about that night you and
your mum went skinny-dipping at the beach!
Remember that fat policeman who almost caught
you, but then got his bike stuck in the sand? You
both ran through the dunes back up to the cottage
holding towels in front of you, leaving him with
undies as his only clue! We must have laughed
until three o'clock before we drove back..."

"...Then he goes on about some other boring stuff."

Lily almost choked on her tea. "Gracious! I don't remember
you telling me about that one, dear. Oh, Henry, don't look so
shocked at my outrageous family. Here, have another cup of tea."

"It's just that my parents don't write letters at all like that," I
stammered. "I don't think they laugh about things that much."
Then again, I thought, they probably don't even know what
skinny-dipping is, and they certainly wouldn't write about it, or
laugh about it, or tell people at tea-time if they did.

"Oh, here's another one," Jennifer interrupted, waving her
letter once again.

"... This morning, at inspection, Miller managed
to stick a sign on the commander's back. As you
know, the old chap is more than a little stuffy.
Well, the sign read:

HANDLE WITH CARE
THIS END UP
(ALWAYS)

With an arrow pointed right at his bum! Well,
there was a terrific row about it. But Miller got
away with it, as there was no way to pin it on him
(so to speak), or any one of the men. Although
the commander was inclined to suspect me…"

Jennifer finished the letter, silently, smiling to herself, the quiet
punctuated by the occasional giggle as she continued to read.
Skinny-dipping? Practical jokes on commanders? I couldn't in a
million years imagine my parents involved in such escapades, or
even thinking about them… let alone owning up to it in a letter.

But here Jennifer was, blurting it all out, unashamedly, sharing
her family fun with us all.

I could imagine her parents enjoying an evening at the table
with us, here in Isleham, laughing and talking. I knew I would
instantly feel at ease with them, too. I wished we could all get
together, and that I could share some extended family time with
Mr. Spitfire Pilot and Mrs. Hush-Hush. Maybe my parents would
even learn to loosen up…

Who was I kidding! I imagined my parents – well, my dad
especially – there at the table. Dr. Doom dampening any warmth
and frivolity with his particular variety of ice. Mr. Respected in
the Community making everybody around him feel uncomfortable
in his presence, uncomfortable even with themselves.

"Henry, be a dear and put the kettle on again, would you?"
Lily's kind voice jolted me out of my reverie. "You seem a little
sidetracked, dear. Are you sure that everything's all right?"

"I'm all right, thanks. More tea sounds great. I'll go put the
kettle on right away…"

I walked into the kitchen and got some more water on the boil.

"I promised Mr. Ned I'd help him in the field again this evening," Charlie said, slipping on his work shoes. "We're setting in some late celery, so I'd better run over there and meet him."

"Gotta love playing with the celery," I joked. "Don't forget about me when it's time to weed."

"It's always time to weed," Charlie shot back.

"Don't let Ned talk your ear off," Jennifer teased. "You know how he goes on so."

"Right," Charlie laughed. "Cheerio then."

"Cheerio."

As Charlie was walking across the road so he could sign up for some more back breaking work with Ned – happily – I settled back into the big sofa with my cup of tea, a halfway-decent book, and some strangely contradictory feelings that left me troubled and uneasy, trying to get comfortable yet not quite managing it.

Jennifer's ancient but dignified Persian cat, Nebuchadnezzar, walked sedately across the back of the upholstery, letting her enormous tail trail behind my neck. The cat paused, looked critically at my lap, and then jumped heavily onto my legs, looking for a scratch behind the ear. I obliged, laying my book down and shifting again to try and get settled.

"If you were a dog I'd take you for a long walk," I told the cat as she stretched her paws across my stomach, eying her claws carelessly as if wondering where to poke, pressing in and out, purring, probing for some hidden prize.

"We could take Newton," Jennifer offered. "That is, if you don't mind a little company?"

"I didn't know a farm dog would take a leash," I said. I was surprised, but pleased that Jennifer would even consider taking a walk with me.

"It's my understanding that Newton was born to a rather snooty town family over in Newmarket," smiled Jennifer. "He only tolerates the farm because he's passionate about the country fresh air."

"Then let's go," I said, putting a marker in my book, quickly slurping the remains of my tea, and sliding off the couch.

*   *   *   *

In a matter of moments we were walking slowly up the quiet lane toward the village, soaking in the country air and the early evening sunlight. Newton tugged at his leash and sniffed, exploring every interesting odor, while Jennifer attempted to get him to walk a partially straight line.

"You never know when Newton might need his manners," she explained. "So I'm trying to teach him a few."

I walked with my hands in my pockets, still feeling ill at ease with my newfound comfort.

It took about ten minutes to reach the center of the village, and we paused at the corner by the Baptist chapel, trying to decide which way to go.

"Do you need to talk, Henry, or do you just need to walk?" Jennifer asked. "You were looking really fidgety there at the end of tea time."

"Am I that obvious? Did it show that much?" I was surprised.

"Call it a calculated guess." She wiggled her eyebrows. "I have ways of paying attention. I have ways of making you talk."

"I dunno," I responded. "Let's just walk up to the village green and let Newton run around a little."

We continued on in silence, enjoying the seventy-degree air and the simple beauty of an early summer evening in the country.

The smell of freshly cut grass wafted over from the parish churchyard, and strains of beautiful pipe organ music made their way through the open doors. Deep from the sanctuary, I could just hear the faint echoes of a lone voice singing along with the evening hymn. Turning left, we approached the spectacular old oaks and chestnuts surrounding the green, its generous acres of lush grass inviting us to stop and sprawl.

"Try laying down on your back and looking straight up," Jennifer said, suddenly throwing herself down, sprawled out on the turf. She was still wearing her school uniform: gray and green plaid skirt, knee-socks half rolled down, white crumpled shirt-tails hanging out. She was - not surprisingly - unconcerned with the propriety of tucked in blouses, adequately covered legs, or stylishly brushed hair.

"You get a whole different view of the world when you look up into the sky," she said enthusiastically.

So I joined her. Newton flopped to the ground, too, his head between his paws, watching us as if we were the ones he had taken for a walk – which was largely true.

The particular chestnut tree we had landed near, rose into my field of vision from somewhere behind my head, spreading out into a magnificent panoply of emerald gems as its arching limbs extended fresh new leaves into the evening sunlight. The sky, framed by the cascading branches, seemed to fill the entire universe, and then some.

"This is breathtaking," I gasped, almost giddy from the view. "What a wonderful way to look at the world."

Newton, suddenly bored, lumbered away to investigate some interesting scent that was calling his name.

"This world is exciting, Henry." Jennifer spoke directly into the air. "The trees, the sky, the people, families - everything."

Her voice spoke of conviction, and of passion, and of belief.

"There are always fresh ways to look at things, Henry. You only need to keep your eyes all the way open – and your imagination turned on."

She rolled over onto her side to look at me, eyes just inches from my face. I could almost feel her breathing.

"And your heart, Henry, you have to keep your heart open, you have to keep your heart turned on too."

I felt pulled in to her deep sense of joy.

"Your family is so... so different from mine." I continued looking straight up, beyond the trees, into the universe. Then I just started talking, and everything inside me kind of poured out.

"I feel like I can communicate more effectively somehow, here in the village with all of you," I said. "I can talk more honestly. I don't know how, but the contrast seems so obvious, and it makes the atmosphere of my home back in Folkestone seem to be that much more stifling, and disappointing, and sad."

I felt, rather than saw, Jennifer nodding her encouragement.

"I've always known something was wrong. It's just that now – being here – I... I can really tell there's a difference. And now I understand more about what might be possible in a family, it makes me feel both good, and not so good, both at the same time."

I hated myself for the way I was stumbling over the words, the way I floundered helplessly around the whole idea. I had this big, enormous feeling inside my heart, and it was coming out of my mouth like a small piece of leftover nothing.

"Go on," Jennifer said.

She was reassuring, and I felt that maybe there was a chance she might understand what was happening inside my head... inside my heart.

"Basically, it's my dad." I kept looking up into the chestnut tree; somehow it made me feel safer. "But I guess it's really more about the way we have all become, including mum, it's about how we are with each other...."

Then I went on to tell her about the conflicts, the lack of communication, the double standards, the yelling. Somehow it all came tumbling out. And I didn't leave out my part, my personal complicity. In fact, as I told her about it, all my own guilt seemed to amplify, and I realized the situation had developed – over time – into a fairly even, fifty-fifty, balance when it came to sharing responsibility.

"But do you know what my greatest wish is?" I said softly, turning on my side too, meeting her gaze directly.

"What?" Her soul seemed to be reaching right out, drawing me in through her eyes. They were dark, liquid, and so very, very deep. It felt natural to talk with her this way, as if I had known her for a very long time.

"I want to hear my dad say, 'I love you,'" I said. "And I want to understand that he means it. That's all. I know it doesn't sound like anything very dramatic, but I really want to feel that he loves me. And I want to believe that I really love him too."

"Sounds to me," Jennifer said, rolling over and sitting Indian style, her long brown legs wrapped around each other like pretzels, "that you really want things to work out with your dad."

"Yes. Yes, I do," I said, not at all sure I had actually realized before this moment how very much I wanted things to be right with my dad. Jennifer's enormous hazel eyes sparkled against the tan of her skin. I don't think that I'd ever seen a girl with skin that golden. Or maybe it was that I'd never before really taken notice of the color of a girl's body.

Jennifer reached out and gently squeezed my hand. "I'm sure you will know what to do," she said, looking all the way into my soul.

"Hey Newton," she suddenly yelled, dropping my hand. "Give those kids their ball back and come on over here. It's time to go home."

CHAPTER FIFTEEN

Get on Your Bikes and Ride!

Being on a farm certainly had its advantages when it came to eating – especially breakfast. Wartime restrictions played a big part, to be sure, but when you grow your own food there is always some that ends up in the farmer's kitchen cupboard, and I was eternally grateful to the chickens that lived nearby for their part in the war effort. I loved eggs.

Meat was another matter. My favorite cuts were going to be somewhere in the range of scarce to non-existent no matter what. But, once a week – Saturdays more often than not – the traditional English farmhouse breakfast always managed to appear on Lily's kitchen table, courtesy of the pigs.

Lily may have delegated the responsibility of raising those peculiar creatures to Jennifer, but I was one hundred percent involved when it came to the eating. So my appreciation goes out to both of them (and whatever agreement they had with the neighborhood butcher who stored and distributed such bounty –

legal or otherwise). Bacon was our most anticipated treat, and I determined that I never wanted to miss another Saturday morning breakfast so long as I was anywhere within a hundred miles of Lily's kitchen.

"What do you think you'd like for breakfast this morning, Henry? A little of everything?" Lily already knew the answer to that question and this was only my fifth Saturday in the village.

"Yes, please," I responded hungrily, walking over to the stove to watch her cook.

"Talk me through it, Lily," I said. "I want to be able to fix this myself one day."

"Well it's all very simple," she started to explain. "First you get a good hot frying pan, preferably a deep one so you don't splatter too much fat everywhere. Then, put in as many big plump rashers of thick meaty bacon as you can spare – none of that thin crispy bacon some people seem to like. Once the fat is sizzling… like this… you just throw in all these other wonderful ingredients. The secret is to keep it moving around. Here, you do it."

"Ow! This is hot," I objected. "Okay, here goes. Tomatoes; mushrooms – I really love mushrooms; sausage; baked beans; eggs."

"Wait on the eggs till everything else is almost done," Lily said as the smell started to get extra delicious.

"Do you have to sell most of your eggs?" I asked.

"Thankfully not," she said. "I only have the ten hens, so they don't have to be officially registered. This way I can give most of my eggs away instead – I prefer that anyway. Now don't forget to keep everything moving around." She looked at the pan full of goodness. "I'd say you're about ready for the eggs."

By now the "mixed grill" aroma was beyond wondrous.

Lily nudged my elbow. "Don't forget the fried bread."

"Like this?" I dropped two thick slices of bread into the pan and they instantly began to soak up all the drippings and the flavor.

"That's right. Now, turn the bread – yes, that's a perfect golden brown – and scoop it all onto this hot plate."

As I carefully followed directions, Jennifer sleepily shuffled into the room cradling a mug of hot coffee between her hands. "Good morning, Granny." She kissed Lily on the cheek. "Hi there, evacuee."

She looked longingly at the generous plate full of hot, fried, yummy breakfast. "Is that mine?"

"If you want it to be," I replied. "All my own work."

"Hey. I'm impressed. Thanks."

"Can I do the next batch by myself?" I asked Lily. "It'll be for you."

"Certainly, but not even half that amount. No, wait a moment. We'll just throw in some extra and ours will cook together. I'll watch you through while I pour us all some tea. This way we can all sit down and eat at the same time."

By the time I had finished the second frying pan full of farmhouse breakfast, I was so hungry I could have eaten right out of the skillet. Jennifer's series of "isn't this yummy" comments while mine was cooking didn't help much. As it was, I only just made it to the table before diving enthusiastically into the assortment of fried breakfast goodness at high speed.

"This isn't half bad," I said.

"For a beginner…" Jennifer teased.

"For even an expert," Lily interjected on my behalf. "You can't make a mixed grill any better than this."

*   *   *   *

We had everything cleaned up and the kitchen shipshape by eight o'clock. Satisfied and full, I opened up the kitchen door and wandered outside to see that it had rained lightly during the night. The new day promised freshness, flooding my senses with the kind of newly washed country-air fragrance some enterprising person should probably bottle and sell in the city. A partly cloudy sky stretched wide and dome-like over the adjacent fields. A slight breeze from the east rustled the leaves, carrying the sound of first-light farm work from the neighboring acres. It was almost the middle of July.

Lily stuck her head through the open kitchen window. "Will you and Charlie be gone all day?"

"That's what we plan," I said. "We've each got about three shillings saved, and we're going to treat ourselves to lunch before we leave Ely. We should be back between three-thirty and five."

"Well, I'll plan a late tea around five-thirty or so." Lily smiled, and disappeared behind the flowered curtains.

I pulled a cumbersome old bike out from the shed, dusting it off the best I could. Fortunately, it had been brand new when Mr. Duncan purchased it about a year before his death. It was still, however, exceptionally heavy and bulky. Jennifer had offered me the use of her much newer model, but I balked at the thought of a "girl bike." Not only did it have no crossbar, but there was a pink basket attached to the handlebars. She had laughed at me, not the least bit offended.

"Ready, Henry?" Charlie came racing into the driveway before screeching to a halt. His was a similar model to mine and must have weighed as much as a small tank.

"Almost. Hey… if it looks… like we have… to be here… much longer… maybe we can… get our own… bikes sent up.

What… do you… think?" I spoke haltingly, my speech punctuated by repeated pumps of air into the bike's tires.

"Definitely," Charlie nodded. "I just hope these old wrecks will hold out all the way there. How far is Ely anyway?"

"Only about ten miles. And the good thing is there's pretty much no inclines to deal with. Flat all the way there, and flat all the way back."

I checked my pockets for change. "Exactly how much money do you have, Charlie?"

"I get nine pence a week pocket-money, and I've not been all that extravagant since a week or so before we left home," Charlie fished around in his pocket. "I promised mum I'd divert a little to savings every week so I've got - let me see - two shillings and eleven pence available, a little over half a crown."

Charlie looked proud of his thrift. "How about you?"

"Okay, let's do the math. Four threepenny bits - that equals one shilling. Then three sixpences – that's another one-and-six, making a half crown in that pocket. Plus seven pennies, three ha'pennies, and a big marble. That's a total of three shillings and tuppence ha'penny. I've got another half crown in my sock drawer, but that's in case of emergency. Not a bad haul between us."

"Excellent," Charlie observed.

"Here's an interesting piece of trivia. My dad says that if my second cousin in the United States got a quarter – that's twenty-five cents American – for his allowance, then it would have about the same buying power as my shilling."

"Interesting. So is that what he gets, twenty-five cents?" Charlie asked me.

"No! His old man gives him one whole dollar, every week."

"Lucky dog. So are you getting a whole shilling now?"

"They just raised it. Used to be nine pence, same as you. But my mum upped it to a shilling when we left. She said the three additional pennies will make up a little for the extra things she would have been getting for me of we were living at home. Plus she says it's just easier to tape a shilling in with her letter. Last week she sent me a half crown for two weeks and said the extra sixpence was a bonus!"

"Sounds like a good deal," Charlie replied. "I'll have to work that logic on my mum and dad next time I write."

We jumped on our bikes, riding purposefully into the village, then on past the ancient parish church to pick up the tiny road that led to the adjacent community of Soham. We could see scattered groups of farm workers cutting hay, clusters of men and women in overalls swinging large scythes in a smooth and practiced rhythm. The light rain from before dawn had already dried off, and the laborers were trying to take advantage of the spell of good weather to get in as much of the crop as they could.

The early going was smooth and easy, with the light following breeze offering a welcome boost. Not to mention the powerful extra fuel provided by such a wonderful breakfast. All told, it had been a good first month in the village, but we were excited to be setting out on an adventure of our own, under our own steam. We made the four or so miles to Soham in good time, around half an hour, then immediately turned northwest toward Ely. We were relaxed, riding at a good pace, our spirits elevated.

Some of the hedgerows stood as high as a small house, and the road meandered around the occasional field, so we were not always able to keep our eyes focused toward our destination. Charlie and I kept up a pretty good pace, aided by the empty road and the balmy conditions. Then, at one point, coming through a deep bend in the road and up a small rise, we found ourselves about two miles away from Ely and with the city in full view. Charlie stopped abruptly.

"Look, Henry," he said. "It really does look like an island."

"Amazing," I said, immediately awestruck at the sight. "And, look, there's the cathedral."

It was beyond spectacular. There in the middle of the low fenland, like the squat hump of a volcanic island rising from the ocean, stood the city of Ely. Fields, trees, low buildings, homes, shops, and then the towering height of the great church rising in a crescendo of definition from the otherwise uninterrupted farmland.

"Remember sitting up on the hills a few weeks ago, looking over to France?" I asked.

"How could I forget? That was the last time we managed to get up there before we were exiled for our crimes."

"You mentioned something about William the Conqueror being the last person to successfully invade England, in 1066."

"That's right," Charlie said with some passion. "Hitler should read his history, get realistic. There's no way he can come over here and win."

"Here's some more history for you," I said, armed with few facts I'd learned from Lily. "Ely is where King Hereward the Wake – *The Last of the English* – held out against William when Mr. Conqueror was ravaging the rest of the country. William may have occupied and crushed at will, but here in the low country, Hereward held out. It was so marshy back then it really was just about as good as an island."

"So, Mr. History Expert," Charlie said, "why is Ely called a city when Folkestone is at least four times the size and we only get credit as a town?"

"It's all about the cathedral," I replied. "In the absence of a cathedral, there is no city. There could be a million people, but it takes a cathedral to make a community count as an official city."

"Or..." Charlie interjected, kind of answering his own question even as he voiced it, "a village of seventy-five people would still be a city if it had its own cathedral?"

"Genius," I said. "You've got it."

"But it doesn't make sense," Charlie wanted to argue.

"Hey, it's as good a rule as any," I shrugged my shoulders. "Anyway, maybe having a lot of noise and people and industry and progress isn't the most critical thing to make a community important?"

Charlie scratched his head. "That's enough! Too much thinking! My brain can't handle any more of this!"

"No argument here," I said. Because the next thing we were going to have to sort out would be, 'What makes one church a church, and another church a cathedral?'"

We rode slowly toward the small city, no longer in such a hurry to cover miles. And it seemed, as we progressed, that the village part grew smaller and smaller, and the cathedral part grew bigger and bigger – until all either one of us could see anymore was the massive church. Pasture, marshland, ditches, levees, the Great Ouse River, and fields loaded with crops came right up to Ely's boundary; over nine hundred years of history and architecture cast its imposing shadow across the entire community.

"Good grief, Charlie," I said as we coasted into the grassy area on front of the cathedral's main entrance. "The only other cathedral I've ever really explored is Canterbury, and it has to deal with being walled-in by those houses and business in the shopping area downtown. This church just comes right up out of the ground and never stops! It's incredible."

We leaned our bikes against an old cannon set in the grass. "We've got an hour or so before lunch," Charlie said. "Let's go in and explore."

"Right." I nodded my head. "This should be really good."

CHAPTER SIXTEEN

A Window Looking Directly into Heaven

The great twin oak doors of Ely Cathedral's west entrance stood wide open, allowing a cool stream of fresh air to pour out into the July warmth. It reminded me of a story in my geography book about the Amazon, and how the mighty river pushes fresh water many miles into the otherwise salty South Atlantic Ocean.

Charlie shivered. "Look at this," he said, incredulous. "I can step in and out of the flow of cool air. There must be at least a ten degree difference!"

The air didn't blow out as if pushed by a fan; it more or less poured into the outdoors, suggesting the vastness of the space, the thickness of the cold stone, the total indifference of the building to the fickle fluctuations of the external climate.

145

We entered the porch, awed already by senses other than mere sight, our natural boyish noise and thoughtlessness quieted even before we noticed the sign that commanded it. Our curiosity was piqued, our sensibilities heightened with each passing moment. When we stepped in we were instantly possessed by a sense of reverence we had not anticipated.

"Let's pick up one of those guidebooks over there," I said, dropping a penny in the box requesting donations for upkeep.

The place appeared completely empty, each careful footfall magnified by the absolute stillness.

"I don't know if we're even meant to be in here, "Charlie whispered. "What if I trip and make a noise or something? I'm almost afraid to move."

"It's all right," I said in a rare moment of theological insight, "you're always welcome in church."

The enormous central hall – the guidebook called it the *nave* – stretched endlessly in front of us, a colossal gorge, a fissure punctuated by enormous columns rising to the vast height of the painted roof. It felt exactly like a deep canyon, except with a lid.

"Good grief Henry!" Charlie pointed to a skillfully illustrated page in the guide. "The roof in here is over seventy feet high. Wow!"

"And the whole place is so full of light!" I wondered aloud.

"Look!" Charlie touched my arm and pointed up, high under the roof. "There's a long row of windows over fifty feet up, and then – see - even more light coming from these side aisles, '*transepts*' it says here. Somehow the light seems to find its way throughout the entire building."

The main part of the cathedral appeared to be built in three distinct levels:

- The widest part, at the bottom, had beautiful, long windows which lit the transepts running each side of the great nave.
- The next level, above the transepts, appeared to be designed for the exclusive purpose of providing more light, which flowed in like water through great archways between the pillars, and into the central nave. The guidebook called this a *clearstory*.
- And then, tucked in under the roof at the narrowest portion of the structure, I could see the windows Charlie had pointed out. They made a third layer of light that threw patterns of sunshine and shade into every crevice of the great edifice.

"I'm going to pace off the middle; it looks like it goes on forever down there."

I let Charlie go on ahead and enjoy his details. He stepped out measurements like an engineer. But I was more interested in the immeasurable – the overwhelming feeling that accompanied simply being in the enormous church. Wandering slowly down toward the center of the building; touching the cold stone pillars; stooping to trace my hands over the worn stone flooring; turning circles, as I tried to walk while looking straight up; feeling, all the way into my heart, the raw power that such immensity represents, the creativity and the work that fashioned such a play of light and strength.

I felt exhilarated by the depth and the glory of it all.

The sheer grandeur of the space was so distracting I ran right into Charlie, who was also looking up by this time. "It…, it has at least five, six, no eight, sides. Wow, it's a hexagon."

"That makes it an octagon, dummy," I said, following his gaze up into the towering roof.

"Here in the guidebook it says the central 'Norman' – that's 'William the Conqueror' Norman – tower collapsed, 'with a roar like thunder,' on February twelfth, thirteen hundred twenty-two. Then, instead of rebuilding it exactly the same way, some guy came up with the idea of this eight-sided tower, seventy-two feet across. That's amazing!"

"Man," I said. "The octagonal part of the structure doesn't even start till over seventy feet up, where the roof of the nave is. Even my limited talent with mathematics tells me that's a really long way up!"

The cathedral was laid out as an enormous cross. The long nave, the choir, and the various chapels behind it, added up to close to five hundred feet in length - that's over one and a half football fields! The cross piece must have been a little more than two hundred feet long. The point at which the two main structural elements intersected had been cleverly changed into another octagon by cutting off the ninety-degree angles with short walls that were equal in measurement. There were, in consequence, four walls set at forty-five degrees, and four open archways (seventy-feet high), with eight massive pillars defining the dramatic space.

I positioned myself carefully and lay flat on my back, looking straight up. I couldn't help but think about Jennifer, and how she would likely have been taking the same approach. We were in the exact geometric center of the great octagon, the mathematical centerpiece of the entire cathedral. The giant pillars soared up into the air, then fanned out in an intricate design that joined together again to create a smaller eight-sided roof.

"Check it out," I whispered to Charlie, who got down on the floor and joined me. "It's like someone cut a hole in the cosmos, and we're looking all the way through and into heaven."

And that's really what it felt like, because the "hole" protruded another sixty feet up into the sky to reveal an octagonal lantern, naturally lit, with eight sets of brilliant windows and thirty-two panels of elaborate paintings.

"Charlie," I found myself whispering because I was, once again, being drawn into the hallowed beauty of the lovely church. "You know what's mysterious about this?"

"No. What? Except that this whole place is beyond incredible? I dunno... maybe having it all to ourselves? Or how old this all is? Or how the people back then even managed to build it, completely by hand, so long ago? It seriously gives me a strange feeling...."

"Right; that's exactly it," I said.

"What?" Charlie wanted to know.

"You said it, Charlie. It's the way this place makes me feel. But a building can't make someone feel, can it? That's what's so uncanny."

"Explain?" Charlie said.

"Well, how does this place make *you* feel?" I asked.

"Unusual," he responded. "Not what I would have thought. I guess I got a hint of it when we were riding over here on our bikes."

Charlie stopped for a moment and looked at me with a curious expression that was a mixture of questioning and at the same time not needing to question, as if he was searching for the same feeling, the thing that I simply could not put my finger on.

"Go on," I said.

"You know how a massive castle makes everything around it look kind of insignificant in comparison? Or how one of those gigantic monuments makes you feel, or how a huge ocean liner like the Queen Mary makes other stuff look like nothing?"

"Yes," I said. "I think so."

"Well, riding up here this morning, I noticed how big the cathedral is. I noticed how small the houses and everything seemed in relation to the massive scale. But here's the thing: they may have looked small, but they didn't look unimportant. They didn't look like they were dominated by the church, instead they looked, well... they looked sort of... I don't know... they looked more... taken care of."

"So?" I said, trying to grasp Charlie's idea.

"So that's how I feel, in this place," my friend explained. "It's how I feel inside. I don't feel small because everything is so grand. In fact, what this church makes me feel is important! You know, if someone like the mayor, or the preacher, or some celebrity takes the time to remember your name, how thrilled you feel? This place makes me think like that, this place makes me feel like I'm somebody after all..."

I didn't know what to say. It didn't seem to make sense in the logical way that things are supposed to. But I understood exactly what Charlie was talking about. In some hard to explain way I saw the same thing he did, and I guess he had said it all as well as it could be said.

"All right then, Okay. Lunch." was all I could think of to say. "How about we find someplace to eat, then come back later?"

"Sure thing," Charlie replied. But we didn't move, we didn't move a muscle, not either one of us. Instead, we just lay there on our backs, looking up, feeling somehow affirmed, peering into our own souls through the eight-sided lantern, gazing into heaven, our eyes beginning to open.

CHAPTER SEVENTEEN

The Wreck & the Rain – the Plot Thickens

We eventually did - reluctantly - drag ourselves away from the massive church in order to hunt down a late lunch. Charlie and I walked about a hundred yards away from the cathedral and found an inviting 𝕺𝖑𝖉𝖊 𝖂𝖔𝖗𝖑𝖉𝖊 storefront café. It was the kind of place that offers nothing much beyond pots of tea, delicious sandwiches, and meat pies. We opted for the pies, very good too, and at sixpence a piece – including a pot of hot tea – we were well satisfied.

And so it was a little past two-o'clock in the afternoon when we finally decided to climb onto our bikes and aim toward our home base in the village of Isleham. We thought about going back to the cathedral, but decided we didn't want to break the mood. Besides, we could ride back another day and explore to our hearts' content.

"After a quiet walk around the cathedral and a meat pie, I think I'm ready for a good bike race," Charlie yelled at me over his shoulder.

"On these old clunkers? I don't think so," I hollered back.

"Just watch me. Try to keep up, slow-poke."

Charlie managed to get off to a fairly good start on the mild slope out of Ely and down into the low fen country that surrounds the city. He got the jump on me, stood up, peddled hard, and was accelerating away from my position before I had time to react. Of course my friend knew from experience I couldn't resist getting sucked into any kind of a challenge. Even so I had a hard time trying to catch up.

"Wait up, Charlie," I yelled, already panting hard. "This is meant to be a relaxing ride."

"Race you to that bridge," he huffed, "then we'll coast."

I still had some distance to make up, but I came progressively closer until I finally caught him, coasting in his slipstream for a moment while I caught my breath. We were still more than twenty-five yards from a squat little humpback bridge that crossed a small stream before a sharp curve in the road.

With one last burst of effort I swung out wide to pass Charlie on the right. "Got you now," I yelled, grinning over my left shoulder as he began to fall behind me.

Suddenly, as I was watching him, a horrified expression came over his face. "Look out!" he shouted.

I turned back around abruptly, just as we crested the steeply humped bridge, I suddenly found myself face to face with a horse drawn cart that had appeared seemingly out of nowhere.

My momentum was already taking me to the opposite side of the road, so I swerved violently to the right, barely missing the startled animal. That's when I conformed to all the laws of physics that pertain to centrifugal force, momentum, impetus, and Murphy's Law, careening over a low embankment and becoming momentarily airborne before landing hard in a field of long grass that was being grown for hay.

"Aaaaarrrrrgggggghhhh!" I howled dramatically, as my bike and I parted company, both coming to rest in the overgrown pasture.

"You all right Henry?" Charlie yelled.

I picked myself up slowly, brushing off dirt, grass, dust, dignity, and who knew what.

"Yes thanks. Let's check out this bike though," I replied. I was shaken, but apparently undamaged.

The horse stopped at the apex of the bridge, quietly surveying the scene while the elderly gentleman driving the cart held onto the reigns. He watched us patiently, quizzically, chewing on an empty tobacco pipe, apparently waiting for an opening to speak.

"Err... sorry if I frightened your horse, sir," I ventured, amazed at the amount of mud and debris I had picked up from the wreck.

"Aye, son," he responded. "Te 'orse'll see sight far worse'n thee, I'll reckon, afore 'e's done with." He looked me up and down slowly, meticulously. "Reckon thou'lt be looking next time thou crosses te bridge."

The horse, obviously cut from the same cloth as his master, gave us both a dispassionate look. The taciturn beast then returned to slowly chewing something he was far more interested in than two speeding teenagers. Eventually, and with barely a perceptible jolt, he started off down the road without even being told.

*   *   *   *

Other than a bent mud-shield, which we straightened with the help of a few swift kicks, the bike was fine. So – after pulling out some clumps of grass and mud – we started off again, determined to enjoy the rest of the ride without any more adventure. The serenity we had achieved in the cathedral had been thoroughly overturned by the excitement. We were both ready for a quiet, relaxing, uneventful ride back to the village.

"No speed, no riding on the wrong side of the road, no acrobatics, and nothing – absolutely nada – in the way of horses," I said. "We've got all the time in the world to get home for Lily's scrumptious tea, and I don't want to get there in an ambulance."

"What about rain?" Charlie said. "You didn't say anything about rain, did you?"

"What are you talking about?" I said.

"Look over there."

I followed his gaze down the long road toward Isleham, where the sky had changed dramatically from deep blue to a soupy gray in a matter of minutes.

"Great," I sighed. "This is just what we need."

About a mile in front of us we could see a black-gray darkness moving up the country road like a thick vapor – which it more or less was. The ground level cloud ate up trees, bushes, and fields like a silently ravenous beast. I had seen storms that moved like this sweep in from the sea back at my home in Folkestone, but this one surprised me, being so far inland as we were. It was like night approaching, but at the wrong time. Everything was quickly disappearing – just a few feet at a time – in a deep and inky kind of blackness.

"Do you see any kind of shelter?" I asked, already knowing the answer.

"Nothing. There's hardly more than two or three trees between here and Soham."

"Not that it matters," I added, "here it is."

Almost immediately, a clear-cut wall of water engulfed us. One moment it was dry, the next we were drenched. Charlie was transformed – suddenly and completely - from a brown-haired boy wearing baggy trousers and a white shirt with sleeves rolled up, into a fair approximation of a drowned rat. Not gradually, not a little at a time, but instantly – as if someone had waved a magic wand. His hair was plastered to his head, his shirt stuck to his body, and his soggy pants clung tightly to his legs. I couldn't help but laugh.

"You look like you just crawled out of the river!" The cool water tasted fresh, dripping down my face and into my mouth.

"You don't look so well-groomed yourself," retorted Charlie, big droplets of rain forming on the end of his nose.

I shivered involuntarily, conscious of the sudden drop in temperature. "Brrrr. It's cold all of a sudden."

"If you stay wet, your body will eventually warm the water to its own temperature," Charlie ventured optimistically, "and you won't feel so cold anymore."

"Where'd you learn that?" I shivered. I was neither convinced nor any warmer for becoming aware of the information.

"Some science magazine I've been reading, very interesting stuff. They say experiments have shown Navy frogmen can swim in extremely cold water so long as they're equipped with the proper wetsuits. When water gets trapped next to your skin it heats up to body temperature. The effect is like insulation. Our shirts won't work so well, but the idea is the same."

Charlie sighed with satisfaction, either to suggest he was indeed as comfortable as his theory suggested, or that he was enthralled with the idea of it. Neither my shivering body nor my waterlogged brains were anywhere near impressed.

Having looked around to confirm the lack of appropriate shelter, we climbed tentatively on our bikes and began to pedal slowly in the direction of our destination. With no sign of any potential abatement in the overwhelming downpour, it was going to be a very long ride.

"I'm still cold, Charlie," I complained loudly. Along with the rain had come enough of a chilling breeze to make my soaking wet shirt seem more like refrigeration than helpful wetsuit. "I don't think your navy frogman thing is working out so well."

So we splashed and squelched our way back through Soham and on to Isleham, the constant stream of mud thrown up from our tires adding a unique decorative accent to our bedraggled appearance. It was still raining heavily when we turned the corner onto East Fen Road.

Still shivering, we stopped our bikes outside Lily's cottage. We were both soaked to the skin, and – if possible in light of the fact that we had already attained complete saturation - getting wetter by the minute.

"It's still more than an hour before Lily gets home," I said. "Want to come in for a quick cup of tea?"

"I think I'll skip it for now," Charlie said, "or at least until I've found some dry clothes." Then he started to laugh again. "Did you know that you look absolutely ridiculous?"

"No different than you," I grinned.

"I'm glad we saw the cathedral in Ely." My friend suddenly looked very serious. "I don't think that I've ever felt quite that way before, not about a church."

I nodded, mirroring his serious expression.

"If we hadn't been there together," I said, feeling the rainfall coming down with even more intensity, "I might not understand what you're talking about. But I have to say, the cathedral was certainly worth the ride over… and even the crazy ride back."

"You bet."

"See you later."

"Cheerio."

I stashed the bike in the back of the garage, leaning it up against the wall where I had first found it. At least all the mud had washed off – me and the bike both. I opened the kitchen door to let myself out of the rain.

*   *   *   *

"Don't even think about taking a single step off that door mat!" Jennifer was standing in the middle of the kitchen, looking me up and down and giggling. She pointed at the wet mud dripping off my shoes.

"You look like someone painted your clothes on you in watercolors… and they ran," she laughed.

"So you expect me to stand here all afternoon until I somehow magically dry?" I responded. Part of me was trying to be at least a little irritated, but the situation was simply too obviously funny for me to do anything but smile.

"Of course not." Jennifer handed me a large paper bag.

"What am I supposed to do with this?" I put it over my head and she laughed again.

"Strip," she explained.

"What!" I responded.

"Don't have a cow," she exclaimed.

"You needn't worry, I won't look," she added when my face turned white and my throat emitted a kind of croaking noise.

But I just stood there, shivering and immobilized.

"Sorry, evacuee, but it's the rules," Jennifer said. "Leave your clothes right here, orders of Gran. It applies to anyone who's more than ninety-nine percent water."

Jennifer watched my feeble attempt at protest. "Don't worry, I'm leaving the kitchen. But I'll throw you a towel. And I promise I'll have my eyes closed."

She left the kitchen and I peeled off my wet clothes as quickly as I could, facing away from the living room. I was nervous every moment that someone would open the kitchen door and catch me in a compromising position. It turns out it's astonishingly difficult to take off wet clothes that are sticking to your skin – especially when you're in a hurry.

When I eventually did manage to make it down to my underwear, the elastic in my briefs caught around my toe and I almost panicked. I teetered in place for a harrowing second or two, nearly losing my balance completely. When they finally came off I turned around, stuffed them in the paper bag, and held it in front of me, feeling foolish.

"Where's that towel!" I hollered. "Someone might walk in at any minute."

"Right here, Henry." The voice came from far too close. "Wrap up in this already, before you catch a cold."

Without warning, a large white folded towel hit me in the face. Jennifer emerged from the sofa, where she had evidently been sitting for Lord knows how long. She then walked straight out of the room without looking back in my direction once.

"I've got a hot bath running for you," she said over her shoulder. "And as soon as you stop being such an exhibitionist I'll be able to put the kettle on for some tea."

A few moments later I was lounging in a delightful tub full of hot water. It certainly had been an interesting day.

My experience at the cathedral with Charlie had been a mixture of unnerving and inspirational - in a really good way. Something profound had certainly occurred; I just wasn't sure exactly what.

The adventure on our bikes had been exhilarating, and I realized how important my friends were to me, Charlie in particular. Then there was Jennifer – I wondered if she had any idea of how much she was beginning to bother me. It sure was confusing.

I sighed deeply. Then, involuntarily, I voiced my thoughts out loud. When I did I surprised myself.

"I wish I could talk to my dad."

Wow, I said, this time inside my head; *I honestly wish that I could.*

ELY CATHEDRAL – 1990

Elizabeth sat on the stone floor carefully. She rolled up her jacket as a pillow, then rearranged her position slightly before cautiously placing herself flat on her back. She looked directly up into the octagonal tower.

"Is this the exact place?" she said, adjusting her camera to take in the unique perspective. "It really is just like a lantern looking into heaven. This is beyond amazing."

"I can't believe you've never been to Ely before!" Henry said. "To me this is one of the most breathtaking cathedrals in all of England."

He looked around, appraisingly, noting the emptiness and quiet. "But then again, maybe I'm glad Ely is still off the regular beaten path for tourists. I don't think I'd want to see this place teeming with sightseers - like Canterbury, or Salisbury, or St. Paul's in London. There's a weighty dignity to the stillness here."

Elizabeth's face was shining with the delight of discovery.

"I'd call it a genuine spiritual gravitas," she said. "I probably haven't been to church more than a handful of times in my life.

The way those television preachers talk has always made me think more of used-car salesmen than God... But here, today... I don't know what it is exactly. But there's something else going on in this place."

       *   *   *   *

The train ride from Folkestone had been an impulsive response to the way Elizabeth found herself being pulled into Henry's story. A couple of phone calls (her boss and the dog-sitter) plus a packed backpack, and she was ready to roll.

"It's up to you," Henry had said. "We can talk here in Folkestone for another day, or we can take the London train. Either way I'm quite sure I don't have any other choice but to follow the trail."

Rolling into Charing Cross Station, easing their way over the River Thames, retelling that part of Henry's story, it had been easy to imagine June of 1940, and the carriage full with anxious schoolboys heading who knew where.

"You honestly don't mind me tagging along?" she had said.

"I enjoy your company," he'd replied. "You ask really great questions. Besides, talking about everything that happened is good medicine. But seriously, you will let me know if you begin to get bored?"

"Bored!" Elizabeth exclaimed. "This is a perspective on World War Two I'd never really thought about before. I could talk with you for days."

"At this rate you just might," he said, smiling.

       *   *   *   *

Later that day, in a café across the street from Ely Cathedral, sipping tea and enjoying buttered scones, Elizabeth caught Henry's eye and held it.

"She actually told you to strip? Right there in the kitchen? And then you did?"

Henry rolled his eyes and shrugged his shoulders.

"At the time – in that moment - I felt like I had absolutely no choice. You had to be there for it to make sense. Besides, she didn't look. Well, I'm pretty sure she didn't."

Elizabeth grinned and shook her head.

"Oh, believe me," Henry said, "it gets more interesting."

"I remember being sixteen," she smiled. "Next stop Isleham?"

CHAPTER EIGHTEEN - 1940

Now I Have to Rethink Everything

Towards the end of a relentlessly hot July, two challenging situations unfolded, both featuring kids who were part of my new group of friends at school over in Newmarket.

We just weren't nearly ready for the war to get this personal, and it caught us completely off guard. As a result, we all found ourselves thinking – or rethinking - just about everything we thought we understood. Thinking, yes, but looking with new eyes too. We were looking with new eyes at almost absolutely everyone, every idea, and every situation.

Here's what happened. Over the previous six weeks we had settled nicely into our new routines. Charlie and I were having a blast. We loved being part of our host families, we were fitting in at school, we found ourselves making new friendships, and we couldn't help but enjoy the community. However, every day that passed without the anticipated German invasion amounted to one more day we retreated into a new complacency. We weren't in the danger zone anymore and – while we hadn't intended for it to happen - we were back, almost, to the same level of *laissez-faire* that had defined our response to the rest of the world during those first few months of the war.

Out here in the country, life was good, stress was down, reports from home were positive, and we were being treated better than we could have hoped for. Once again, it was difficult to see the war as anything capable of directly impacting us and our routine lives.

But, at the same time and without our consciously realizing what it meant, more than a few subtle changes were beginning to mount up:

- Bombing raids were increasing all over England.
- There were more and more news stories about the danger facing the convoys of supply ships coming over from America. They were vulnerable, and they were coming under regular attack.
- My mother's weekly letters were beginning to break from her more routine tidbits of rationing, neighbors, church, and friends - now she included reports of shelling, and dogfights over or around Folkestone.
- The dogfights, which had first been noted in late June, had picked up significantly in early July. That much at least caught my interest and attention.

Apparently the German air force – officially known as *the Luftwaffe* – planned to clear the skies of pesky British fighter planes before the Supreme Command launched their anticipated attack on England. Hitler wanted victory in the air before the vulnerable troop-carrying landing craft attempted any kind of invasion.

Enemy planes were now bombing England's air bases and factories relentlessly, attempting to soften the defenses, trying to shoot down as many Spitfires and Hurricanes as possible, working toward the domination of the skies, putting on the pressure as best they could.

Since July 10, action in the air over the southern counties had increased to the extent that the newspapers had started to refer to the ongoing air contest as "The Battle of Britain." Jennifer's father, the epitome of the classic fun loving, relaxed, daredevil, Royal Air Force pilot, claimed he was having a holiday in the skies.

Maybe it was the casual sense of *jois de vivre* Mr. Spitfire Pilot infused into his letters, but how could we worry all that much when we had our own personal hero, someone who was having so much fun shooting down so many enemy planes? He was already an "ace" fighter pilot, just a few weeks into the current escalation; according to him it was like taking candy from a baby.

"Our Spitfires are so superior," he wrote, *"poor Jerry doesn't stand a chance."*

The details he carefully failed to worry us with, of course, concerned the overwhelming odds RAF pilots were facing, the shortage of trained aviators (Jennifer's dad was considered a little old for the job himself, but insisted he was nowhere near ready to leave the fray), the urgent need for ramped up aircraft production, and the cumulative lack of sleep.

"Those are mere details!" he'd have said if challenged on the numbers and the complications. "We've got Jerry on the run and he knows it."

*   *   *   *

But then, like I said, something happened at school one week, and the troubling incident radically challenged – and forever changed - the false comfort level we were all beginning to develop.

Actually, it was two things. Or, rather, two boys – first Trevor, and then Abraham.

Trevor Mersey was one of the new friends Charlie and I had made since switching over to the Newmarket school's morning class schedule. His dad was an experienced merchant seaman, a career officer involved in running cargo through the U-Boat *Wolfpack* blockades in the North Atlantic. His family lived in Liverpool, but Trevor had been sent to Newmarket to stay with his aunt for the duration.

Trevor found his way to the school around six months ahead of our Folkestone group. He was essentially in the same situation as us, he just didn't bring his entire school with him. As a recent newbie, he'd gone out of his way to make both of us feel welcome. He escorted us around the campus, showed us the ropes, and took some of the edge off the transition. Consequently, we'd become friends.

One day we got the terrible news that Trevor's dad's ship had gone down, blown out of the water with only a handful of men surviving. Apparently, two torpedoes had struck the transport in the vicinity of the engine room. Whatever cargo had been carried on board – and it was not out of the question to mix munitions with shipments of food and other domestic supplies – ignited with amazing ferocity into a spectacular fireworks display. The vessel had been blown into a million pieces. The bridge, eyewitnesses on one of the escorts reported (the exact place where Trevor's dad had undoubtedly been stationed at the time) had vanished instantly in a white-hot ball of fire so intense observers had been forced to shield their eyes,

This was not the first time the extended school community had been touched by a death, but Trevor was the first student to lose a parent in direct wartime hostilities. It was a stunning blow, to be sure. But what affected us the most was the way that it destroyed Trevor so publically, right there in the school. It changed the rest of us on a gut level, and it brought the reality of the horrors of war into the insulated cocoon of our day-to-day routines.

Trevor insisted on coming to classes, just the day after the news came out, even though he had been excused. He told the rest of us he didn't think he could make it if it wasn't for his friends; he said that he needed us to help him get through. Then he stood right there in the front of the class and cried, unabashed, asking for our help.

But we were all far too immature to be the rocks he needed us to be, and we honestly didn't know what to do; so most of us reacted by being embarrassed, and ashamed, and distant. It was a lot for Trevor to ask, and we did not have it in us. When it became obvious we were going to fail him, Trevor walked around the school for the rest of the week in conspicuous grief, broken and depressed, head down, shuffling his feet.

Trevor had said we were the friends he needed, and he told us he would be lost without us. Then, after we failed to step up, he gradually fell to pieces as we all continued to let him down.

I think we all knew it was too much to expect. Even the adults - too caught up in their own reaction to the war to give us any useful guidance - were detached and distracted in their own way. None of us had the emotional wherewithal to offer the kind of friendship Trevor's loss demanded. We didn't understand why he didn't know that, and he didn't understand why we were so withdrawn.

The last time I saw Trevor was the day his mother finally came down from Liverpool to fetch him. But it was too late. They had to come to the classroom and escort him to the school office. By then he was the most pitiful blob of sadness we had ever known. Our friend was lost and broken, and we had quickly learned to steer clear.

None of us were prepared or equipped for Trevor's loss, including the teachers and staff. And no one seemed to grasp that this was just the beginning of the torrent of grief to come.

*   *   *   *

If we weren't ready for Trevor, then at least it was because of Trevor we found ourselves more prepared for Abraham. Abraham Cohen showed up at our school the very next day, and maybe it was our guilt and grief about Trevor that made it possible for us to listen to our new friend. He was a friend, it turns out, who had quite the story to tell.

Abraham was a genuine refugee from another country. And because of that, he achieved instant celebrity status. He was staying with the local Presbyterian minister and his family, waiting for his father and some other relatives to make it out of Austria, where the family had lived for generations. Fifteen years old, extremely smart, pitch perfect English, very articulate, he didn't mind talking about his situation and – amazingly (thankfully) – he was nowhere near defeated by it.

Our refugee student was able to put flesh and bones on a narrative we were only getting bits and pieces of, third or fourth hand, filtered through adults and government censors. He told us things that we would never have guessed.

We were all glad Abraham willingly shared his story. But his authenticity, his audacity, and the powerful way he described the terrible events (especially the ease with which the tragedy unfolded) scared the living daylights out of us!

"No kidding? These people really were your neighbors?" I asked, incredulous. "These same people were your friends?"

"Indeed they were." Abraham's English was very bookish, and he used almost no contractions in his speech, having been taught by his father through years of required reading from classic Nineteenth Century novels.

"But how can people you know and trust just turn on you like that all of a sudden?" one of the boys asked, quickly and easily forgetting the way we had all let down our friend Trevor.

Abraham sighed, as if trying to decide how much to tell. Then he shrugged his shoulders, deciding to take the plunge.

"You really had to have been present to feel the pure evil that can reside in the heart of a mob," he said. "And I am glad that none of you have ever seen anything that would help you to understand."

We were in a "private study hall" class session. There were no teachers present, and the boys in the room started to gather round Abraham to listen.

"Listen, I don't intend to frighten you, but it was like this..." You could have heard a pin drop. "I was at my bedroom window, observing the mob as it moved down my street. They moved through the merchant district one night after a big Nazi rally in the town square. The people smashed the windows of every store marked with the yellow star that identified us as Jews. At first they had been encouraged by the SS, but after a while the crowd managed to get along well enough under its own steam."

He paused, collecting his thoughts. "I saw my friends Frank and Dietrich. They ran over towards our shop. We all grew up together; we were neighbors and best friends since I could remember. I thought they had come over to help, or maybe give me some encouragement until things settled down. But I was so very wrong."

Abraham took another quiet moment, shaking his head as if still experiencing disbelief over what had transpired.

"You have to understand how it was," he told us. "Our store was a much loved location for people to enjoy confectionary, tea, and coffee. We had a few tables in the front, and it was everyone's favorite place to go.

"Mother and father were always so generous. They were generous not only with the children of the town, but with their parents too. Before the days of the yellow star we were the number one gathering spot. Everyone came to 'Cohen's.'"

Abraham stopped talking again. By this time there were more than ten boys gathered around, and I could see the thoughts racing through each head, the furtive glances to friends, the wondering about what loyalty really meant when the chips were down.

"It was Frank who first caught my eye," he continued. "So I waved, making a motion to him that I would meet him round back. I was optimistic. Frank was, after all, my friend. But everything changed in that instant, and I saw something in his eyes that frightened me. He drew back his arm, yelled, 'Filthy Jew boy!' as loud as he could, then sent the first brick crashing through the front window.

"Immediately, a deluge of missiles smashed up the front of our little store. My mother, God bless her, was sitting in front of the counter, confident no one would abuse the generous friendship she has always offered to her neighbors.

"My father immediately rushed in to fetch her away, but he was hit in the head by a brick and dropped, unconscious, behind the counter. He was out of sight and soon forgotten in the heat of what happened next. You see, fear and hate are powerful forces, and there was no stopping the crowd once they had tasted blood."

Abraham gathered himself, pausing for a handful of very long seconds.

"Two men," he continued, "Mr. Brett and Mr. Muller - men whose children had been some of my mother's favorites - grabbed her and dragged her into the street...."

"What did you do?" Charlie interrupted, his mouth hanging open in disbelief.

"I was completely stuck, immobilized," our new friend admitted. "The word is 'petrified' and petrified literally means *unable to move,* or *changed into a stony substance.* It was as if I was paralyzed from the neck down. I watched from my bedroom window. I did not want to look, but I was truly incapacitated, my gaze rooted on what was happening. Then our neighbors, good men I thought, who had enjoyed food and friendship at our kitchen table on many occasions, tied my mother by her feet and hung her upside down from one of the street lamps."

Abraham turned away from us for a moment, looking through the window into the middle distance as if trying to grasp hold of some recollection... or maybe the opposite, to let a memory go.

We listened with growing horror, repelled and fascinated all at the same time, revulsion mixed with curiosity. We didn't want to know the rest of the story, but we couldn't draw ourselves away from the awful truth that was unfolding right in front of us.

"The two men stepped back," Abraham continued, "and then they all just went berserk..."

Abraham paused for a moment or two... stopped, really. There was nothing else to say, there was nothing else he really could say. A little while later he shrugged his shoulders and offered a conclusion. "When my father regained consciousness it was far beyond too late. We left later that night."

CHAPTER NINETEEN

A Birthday and a Pile of Confusion

Early Sunday morning, July twenty-first, I woke up about the same time as the sun. I remembered it was my sixteenth birthday. I crept out of the house, stretched, then took a walk down the quiet country lane that led to the river that runs near the village. The Lark, a tributary of The Great Ouse, is one of the countless waterways and ditches that drain the soggy fens.

It felt strange to be anywhere other than home on a birthday. Home, strained though the relationships had become, was still home. And birthdays had a way – usually – of bringing the family together, of working to ease the tension. Helping at least, if not necessarily healing.

My dad, usually the first up, had always marked birthday mornings with the time-honored tradition of a cup of tea in bed. This was the first time I'd started a birthday without him, and I thought about the unusual tenderness and love with which he woke me, wished me a happy birthday, and left the steaming mug of tea beside my bed.

It was so unlike him, I thought, yet I wished so much that he had been there with me for my sixteenth. Time, after all, was not working in our favor. The truth was that I could not automatically expect many more birthdays at home, even if things went well. After all, what with the war and the unprecedented catastrophic upheaval, I was beginning to realize there might not be any more birthdays. Not at home, not here, maybe not anywhere at all.

I turned and started to walk back toward the village, unbuttoning the light jacket I had put on to ward off the early morning chill. The rising sun gradually illuminated the sprawling fields. Unbroken acres of ripening wheat stretched endlessly around me. Just a few more weeks of good sunshine, and then it would be time to crank up the harvester so Ned could begin the dawn to dusk process of bringing in the crop.

A variety of farming sounds told me the rural community was slowly beginning to respond to the less urgent call of a Sunday morning. Roosters crowed much as any other day. Cows reminded their owners they were anxiously waiting to be milked, mooing their impatience. Birds poured out their enthusiasm for life in song. Dogs woofed to be let out, or let in. One bark, though, made its way closer and closer, until Newton scurried around the corner of the lane, tail wagging furiously, eager to have even a short walk with his new friend, wishing me a very sincere happy birthday in his own way.

"Here boy," I called, squatting down to pat his head and rub his shaggy back. "I wonder if anyone else knows what special day this is?"

I sighed, watching the shadows, long and distorted in the early light. It was not the first time I had thought positively about my dad in the past few days, and it seriously unnerved me. Was I just getting sentimental? Had I been misreading him too much? Was there potentially more to our relationship than being a hot-headed teen had allowed me to consider?

I watched Newton run around me with uninhibited enthusiasm. He jumped up excitedly and stuck his wet nose into the palm of my hand. "Things sure have been rough with dad recently, Newton," I said out loud. "But I don't want them to be. I really wish I felt as comfortable with him as I do with Lily, and with Jennifer. But every time we're together, we just clash."

Newton watched me with those big black dog eyes that always seemed to be packed full with sympathy, knowing, and real understanding.

"Woof. Rowoof," he replied: *I wonder if you would have got your cup of tea this year?* It was a good question. But I was convinced I knew the answer already.

We walked back to the house together, and this time he stayed at heel, looking up at me every two or three seconds as if he wanted to make sure that everything was all right.

*　　　　*　　　　*　　　　*

When we sat down for breakfast, no one even mentioned my birthday. I looked around carefully, scrutinizing expressions and movements for some giveaway that maybe Lily or Jennifer knew. But I was unsuccessful.

Even Charlie, who often came over for Sunday breakfast, seemed to have forgotten this was July twenty-first. I quickly logged that incriminating fact in my brain, under the section entitled, "Catalogue of serious crimes against your best friend." Hadn't I treated him to a movie, and given him a book all about his favorite football team March thirty-first, the day he had turned sixteen?

I smashed the top of my boiled egg viciously, savaged its insides with a spoon, stirred my hot tea so harshly some of it spilled, and tore into the toast without mercy. Nobody seemed to notice I was even there.

Then I saw it, leaning up against the marmalade. It was a small envelope with my name on it, stamped and postmarked a few days previously. "Save until July 21," inscribed above the address. The handwriting was my father's.

Dear Henry:

May I be the first to say, a very happy sixteenth birthday to you. I trust that you have a cup of tea handy when you read this, because I am distressed not to have had the opportunity to bring you one upon awakening this morning. Please consider this a coupon, of sorts, redeemable at the very earliest opportunity, for one morning cup of tea.

Henry, I am also distressed that we have had such a difficult time communicating with one another lately. Maybe, through this difficult time in our nation's history, we will both learn the true value of family, and learn to appreciate one another more.

May I also inquire after your school work? How are you faring regarding your problems with French language studies? Your mother suggests that it might be to your advantage that I am not in a position to pursue this line of query on a daily basis! That, however, is a question that only your school report can answer. I expect excellent marks regardless, as I am sure that you understand.

My regards to the estimable Mrs. Duncan.

Your mother sends her love. I remain, Henry, your affectionate father.

I read and reread my father's letter several times. "Well, what's the news, Henry?" Lily called out from the kitchen. "I don't remember that we've seen a letter from your father before?"

"Oh, nothing much," I replied cagily. "He just wanted to let me know he hadn't forgotten to check up on me."

"Nothing much" was not what I was really thinking, however. It was not merely unusual to receive mail from my father, but downright unprecedented. My mother was always the one to write, and the way she referred to his greetings left little doubt (in my mind) that those had been added by her, just to make me feel like my dad was asking. My understanding had been that he usually wasn't even aware that she was writing. But this time? This letter did not add up. This was an authentic letter from my actual father.

"Hey, Jennifer," I said.

"Humph?" she relied, her mouth full of warm bread and marmalade.

"Would you please read this? And not out loud, but to yourself. And keep it kind of quiet please."

"Right. Hand it over then."

"Here."

She read the letter slowly, pausing briefly only to take a long draft of her enormous mug of morning coffee. When she had finished, she put the paper down carefully, fixing me intently with her huge brown eyes.

"Are you Henry Bradley?" she asked, quizzically.

"Yes. Duh," I replied, not really catching her drift.

"Are you aware that the man in this letter is pretending to be your father?"

"Okay, knock it off," I said.

"Henry," she went on, "that doesn't sound quite like the Dr. Doom you've been describing."

"No," I responded, "it certainly does not."

I folded the letter carefully, and placed it in my pocket.

C HAPTER TWENTY

When a Bumblebee Gets Loose in Church

The Duncans attended church on a semi-regular basis, walking into the village for services at the small Protestant chapel just off the main street. Unlike the Romanesque stone Anglican building, which made for a picturesque scene in the middle of an ancient graveyard, Lily's church was a simple structure where form was obviously a distant second to function.

"Don't you think that some of these people are a little stuffy?" I whispered to Jennifer as we slid down the hard wooden pew to our place, halfway down the left side of the church, underneath a plain, undecorated window.

"No," she replied, a sly smile partially escaping her lips, "I think that all of these people are significantly, over the top, quite a lot stuffy."

An elderly gentleman was playing a painfully discordant version of "When the roll is called up yonder" on the squeaky organ, grating a dismal concoction of vaguely related notes, with the kind of tempo usually reserved for games of musical chairs at nursing homes. I suspect that he was quite deaf.

"When the roll really is called up, he'll either miss hearing it altogether, or he won't make it to the bus," Jennifer snickered as quietly as she could in my right ear. I could sense a subtle hint of perfume as her face almost touched mine, and I had to fight off an urge to lean close enough to make her lips brush my cheek. But then, unexpectedly, a small laugh escaped from my throat, and I choked.

"Don't get me started," I warned. "If I start to giggle, it's ten to one I won't be able to stop. I've been kicked out of more school events for, 'Bradley can't control himself in public' than I could possible count!"

I looked around the church. Somewhere around thirty-five people sat in the ten rows of hard wooden benches that would have held somewhat more than a hundred when full. Everybody seemed to be grouped in small or extended family units. And, while there was a fair sprinkling of all ages, the almost complete absence of young men left a profound impression on my mind.

Eventually, and thankfully, the organ noises stopped. A handful of severe looking men emerged from a door behind the pulpit. Four of them shuffled to seats on the front pew, while the fifth – evidently the preacher – climbed the steps and glared at us all for a few moments before launching into what must have been his opening prayer.

Just as the minister completed his first sentence, there was a shuffling noise at the back of the church. I looked over my shoulder to witness Charlie and his host family creeping as quietly as they could down the aisle. They needn't have bothered with the tiptoeing, because the minister wasn't about to get under way again until they were settled. He stopped in mid-sentence and shook his head disapprovingly, following them all the way to their pew (which was directly in front of us) with a withering look that more than punished them for their tardiness. The scowl may well have taken two or three years from their lives.

Things went pretty smoothly after that, and we thought that we were in for an uneventful hour. Until, that is, the almost exact middle of the preacher's sermon, which was when an extremely large bumblebee made its way through an open window and into the church. That's when things began to get interesting.

The church organist, who did turn out to be deaf, had tottered down from his bench and was seated with his family to listen to the preacher's message. He was obviously quite taken with the progress of the bee, craning his head every which way to follow the insect's circuitous flight, as it meandered around the room, looking for somewhere appropriate to land.

I tapped Charlie on the shoulder. "If we're lucky, that bee will sting the preacher, and maybe we'll get out early."

"No such luck," Charlie replied. "The way he's flapping his arms, there's going to be no way the bee could safely get anywhere near him."

Lily bopped me on the knee just about the same time Ned began to look at us sideways. "Shhhhh...."

The bee, evidently confused, began taking runs at various elaborate hats, only to find nothing sweet enough. The owners of the hats were becoming nervous, people could be seen looking anxiously over their shoulders, and the occasional murmur of muffled conversation wafted over from several locations around the church. Meanwhile the preacher, aware of some competition for his message, upped both the volume and the tempo of his delivery, even accentuating the occasional point with a thump of his fist on the wooden podium.

The battle of the bee, thus enjoined, seesawed momentarily in favor of the minister. But the bee was not to be outdone. "Look," Jennifer whispered to me, "It's gone and landed on Mrs. What's-her-name's neck."

Sure enough the bee, having settled on the shoulder of Mrs. What's-her-name to get a better look at the extraordinary hat, had crawled on over to the apex of one of the folds in her voluminous neck, where the curious insect intently studied a large mole – maybe with the intention of extracting nectar. What might possibly happen next was anybody's guess, and without a doubt much more interesting than the preacher's lackluster sermon. All eyes turned to the second pew.

Again, the earnest preacher sensed an ebb in the give and take of hard won attention, and again – summoning resources from deep within himself – he fought back to reach the critical, decisive, climactic moment of his sermon with, once more, the majority of his parishioners on board.

But it was then, at the exact moment the question hung once more in the balance, at the precise instant that the minister felt that his exhortations were finally falling upon fertile ground, possibly taking root, that the church organist – a full two rows behind Mrs. What's-her-name – stood up suddenly, swinging the entire matter inexorably in favor of the bee.

"Don't worry, I've got it!" the organist bellowed, overcome by an impulse to chivalry. He declared his intention with the inflated volume of one who feels that everyone else has a hearing problem, because they don't talk loudly enough for him. So, with his guarantee of success echoing round the room, the enthusiastic septuagenarian lunged across the empty pew with a rolled up newspaper and swatted, hard, at the peacefully grazing bee.

The organist's aim was not as good as his promise, and all he managed to accomplish was to knock Mrs. What's-her-name's hat off her head, startling the bee, who proceeded to sting the mole. The owner of the mole screamed, the valiant organist lost his balance and fell over the pew, the minister – for once in his long career – was speechless, and Lily of all people began to give in to a *can't-hold-this-back-any-more* giggle.

It took the combined efforts of three people to get the church organist back into an upright position. It took at least five others to calm down Mrs. What's-her-name. But Lily, who gradually submerged into a deep river of mirth, tears running down her face, never could stop laughing.

Eventually, with everyone else edging back toward decorum and the closing hymn finally announced, Lily simply whispered, "See you at home," snorted a couple more times, and made her way out of a side door, her entire body vibrating with hilarity.

I looked at Jennifer. She squeezed my hand. "Happy birthday, Henry," she said. And I didn't fail to notice that by the end of the hymn, she still had not let go.

C HAPTER TWENTY-ONE

"Summer Pudding" and other Surprises

There was to be a birthday celebration, after all. Neither the Duncans nor Charlie had mentioned anything at breakfast, because they intended for the occasion to be a proper surprise. Lily used her head start to fix an extra special lunch, and there were small presents from her, from Charlie, from my parents (who had sent them via Lily), and even from Jennifer, who gave me a tea mug with a Spitfire on it.

Dessert, though, was hands down the best part of all. Instead of a traditional birthday cake, Lily made an interesting concoction that Jennifer simply called, "The Best Thing Ever." There, arranged on the top and spelling out "H.B." – kind of – were sixteen candles. It was spectacular.

"Now that looks really appetizing," I exclaimed. "So what exactly is it?"

"Summer Pudding," Lily replied.

"Because she can only get all the right delicious ingredients in the summer," Jennifer added. "It's scrumptious, it's the absolute best, and my mouth is very excited about the prospect of eating it all up!"

"Sounds better than good," I said. "But I still don't know what it is?"

Lily smiled at her granddaughter. "I know you're dying to give Henry another cooking lesson," she said.

"Well, first, it's all about bringing out all the lovely juices in all the summer fruit," Jennifer said. "That means we put some water and sugar in a large pan, heat till the sugar dissolves, bring it to a boil, tip in some blackberries, redcurrants, and raspberries, and then cook it all together till the fruit is soft. You put a strainer in a bowl, tip in all the juice and fruit, and set it aside."

I started to laugh. "You sound like one of those cooking shows on the radio," I said.

"Then maybe I should be on the BBC?" Jennifer looked serious for a moment, seemed to weigh her career options, and then continued.

"Next you cut the crusts off some white bread, and trim the slices to fit the insides of a large basin. Dip a whole piece of bread into the juice bowl, and set it in the bottom of the basin – that's the anchor. After that you do the same with the other bread pieces and press them around the sides so they fit neatly together. Finally, spoon in all that softened fruit, not forgetting to mix in some yummy strawberries too."

"Did you do all that before lunch?" I asked.

"Yesterday," she said. "Overnight gives all the built-in yumminess more time to set properly. Now stop interrupting and listen to the rest of the cooking lesson.

"After it's full with the fruit you make a juice-soaked bread cap and seal it off. Then you put a close-fitting lid on the basin, and chill the pudding overnight. Voila!"

Jennifer looked proud of herself. "A few minutes ago I flipped it over onto a plate. As you can see Lily likes to serve it with any extra berries and – my absolute favorite – custard!"

With that Lily cut four generous slices of the pudding and covered them liberally with the hot yellow custard that screamed out for an accompanying cup of tea. I was not to be disappointed.

I felt wonderful. A little indulgence, after all, can go a long way – especially when there's a war on and being spoiled is the farthest thing possible from the standard routine.

Lily wouldn't let me help clean up the dishes. I had just finished a second helping of the amazing summer pudding, and the big mug of hot tea was exactly right for the occasion. And – to top it all off – my dad had actually written me a halfway friendly letter - more than halfway. So far, and compared to how low I felt on my early morning walk, this was looking like a most excellent sixteenth birthday celebration.

Charlie made his way back to Mary and Ned's to work on some correspondence, Lily retreated to her room for a long nap, and Jennifer made us a fresh pot of tea. She then plunked herself down on the sofa at a ninety-degree angle to me, balancing her mug on her lap.

"No coffee this afternoon?" I observed.

"I've decided to become equal opportunity," she replied. "Eclectic is the featured vocabulary word this week, and I believe that it fits me well."

"If I knew what eclectic meant maybe I'd agree," I laughed.

Jennifer fished a small notebook from her purse and cleared her throat. "Eclectic: Deriving ideas, style, or taste from a broad and diverse range of sources," she said, smiling. "It's me all over. Diverse, stylish, tasteful, full of ideas."

"Couldn't have said it any better myself," I smiled back.

Jennifer worked her left foot into the space between the sofa and my back. It felt kind of nice.

"So, evacuee, what are you going to do about your dad?" she asked with characteristic directness.

I was nonplussed. This situation was far too difficult to actually do anything about. "I don't know. What do you think?"

"Well, if it was my dad, and I felt this far away from him, it would be killing me," she said. "I'd probably hitch a ride with the first truck I found going to Kent, and we'd talk it out."

"What do you mean, 'talk it out?'"

"Exactly what it says," she said. "Talk. It. Out. Or are you so used to avoiding saying whatever it is that's on your mind you wouldn't even know how?"

Jennifer sighed deeply and shook her head in my direction, as if I'd disappointed her terribly.

"Help!" I said. "I haven't even done anything yet and already I'm in trouble?"

"You know," she said, ignoring my appeal for clemency, "you could simply start by writing a nice thank you letter for the pen and pencil set, and then you could just go on and tell him – honestly – how it is that you are feeling about everything."

I must have looked doubtful, because she started to laugh. "It's not that difficult, Henry. Just give it a try,"

"But I have no idea where to start."

Jennifer sat up straight and gave me an exasperated look. "Start with the 'thank you' letter. Then, just keep talking. Imagine that your dad is listening to you, and write down what you would want to say if he was sitting right here on this sofa, sipping the tea that he had made for you, special for your birthday. And imagine that you were talking as if you weren't even a little bit nervous."

She settled back into the cushions.

"Look," she said. "I'm right here with you. If you want me to read some of it, then fine. If you don't, then that's fine too."

Jennifer curled up snugly into her corner of the sofa, opening the book she had been reading. Nebuchadnezzar, sensing an opportunity, glided gracefully down into her lap and curled his tail carefully around her leg. Jennifer let her hand ease gently down the fluffy Persian's back, and the cat's engine turned on immediately, adding verbal contentment to my silent pleasure – both of us very pleased that our favorite girl was right there.

I sipped my tea guardedly, wondering what to do, and I soon felt a bare toe dig softly at my leg. I looked up to see that I was being scrutinized intently from over the top of Jennifer's tea mug. "Well...?" she questioned.

"Well what?" I replied, knowing exactly what she was getting at.

"Duh! It's not as if your parents didn't give you anything to write with for your birthday. It's not as if that nice new pen isn't sitting right there on the coffee table in front of you. And it's not as if Charlie didn't give you some perfectly good writing paper that would work really nicely with that pen you're holding in your hand. Well...?"

"Okay, okay, okay already. Here goes nothing."

I picked up the writing supplies and worked my way back into my corner of the sofa. Where to begin?

Dear Dad:
    Well, if you're surprised to see this letter, then I'm sorry. I guess that we have both been a little rough on

each other lately. Sometimes I don't feel connected to you at all. So then I don't write, because – well – what would be the point? Of course when I think about it like that, it doesn't make sense or sound fair. But anyway, thanks for the pen and pencil set, I'm using them now. Well, the pen part at least.

Dad. Believe it or not, I was actually thinking about that cup of tea in bed on my walk this morning. I was up early and out with the dog, and I was thinking that I missed having you bring it to me. So I guess we must be connected after all.

I'm having a good birthday so far. Everyone here really makes me feel "at home." I would like to see you, if that's at all possible. I know you are very busy.

Please write again.
Love,
      Henry.

"So, what do you think?" I tossed the letter over Jennifer's novel; it floated gently into her lap.

She read slowly, looked up at me once with those deep, bright eyes, leaned over to where I was sitting, placed the letter back in my hands, and kissed me – warmly – on the cheek.

"You really are quite remarkable," she whispered. "I think that you and your dad are going to be all right. You'd better mail it while it's still hot."

"I need to take a stroll anyway, after all that summer pudding," I said. "Want to come too?"

"All right, it is your birthday after all. We'll pick up Charlie, swing by the main post box, and have a real walk."

Jennifer slipped on her shoes, ran for the door, and tossed a sly smile over her shoulder. "You wouldn't want to be spending all of your time alone with a girl!"

CHAPTER TWENTY-TWO

An Afternoon with Jennifer

The next day happened to be a school holiday. Having the treat of a day off - right after my birthday - turned out to be exceptionally good timing. Consequently, I was more than thankful for the opportunity to luxuriate in the flush of good feelings I had enjoyed the previous day.

First there was the letter that was making me rethink everything I had been assuming about my dad, and then there was the walk home from church, holding hands with Jennifer all the way. I could still feel the peck on the cheek she'd given me Sunday afternoon, after I had put my writing supplies to good use. And finally there was the fact that it felt so good to realize I could respond to my dad's affirming overtures in a positive way.

Both schools needed a full day of teacher planning, as well as an administrative strategy session designed to work out some kinks in the details that made the whole, "let's share the building" cooperation project a ton of extra work for the staff.

The Ministry of Education people had come up with the idea that implementing an overlapping "games" session might help to bring the two school communities together. Plus, there were a bunch of library related logistical concerns, a couple of lunch issues, and some academic details that went along with two schools using the same building at two ends of the same day.

Then there was the headache of rescheduling the big end-of-year exams (the comprehensive testing that would determine the content and direction of our final two school years, and our trajectory toward university). The exams typically took place in June, but were now slated for the middle of August at the earliest.

I could not, personally, have cared less about the details of my education. Charlie and I were in the unique situation of enjoying Isleham all to ourselves, so they could keep all the stressful school complications over there in Newmarket, and we could delight in country life with Lily and the rest of our new friends.

Exams would happen, we understood that, it was one of these immutable laws of being a teenager. We'd even do our best, when everything was ready, and we would deal with it all just as soon as that time arrived.

*   *   *   *

After I had enjoyed a somewhat lazy morning, one that involved reading, cleaning my room, and then harvesting a few vegetables for Lily, Jennifer flounced into the living room and stood over me, swinging two shopping bags and sporting a big smile. I had just got into the second chapter of a promising new novel, and tried to look too comfortable to care.

"Time to get off your duff. You're coming with me, evacuee," she grinned.

"What's up?" I replied, curious but not all that anxious to leave my book.

"It's your birthday treat, day two. This is my real present, and I guarantee you'll love it."

She had my attention. I put the book down.

Jennifer threw one of the canvas bags at me. "Shove your book in here, mine too, and grab the paper bags and the thermos on the kitchen table. I have the absolute best place to enjoy a picnic lunch and then read all afternoon."

"Okay...." Now I was seriously curious.

"Me, and you," she continued. "No one else gets to come. It's can't miss for two confirmed readers slash serious picnickers. Besides, I am beginning to believe we appreciate each other's company enough that riding out on our bikes and enjoying the afternoon would be a great way to spend the day off."

I certainly couldn't argue with that!

So we pulled out the bikes. Jennifer dropped some supplies into her big basket, and I tied the bag I was carrying to the pannier in the back of mine. By this time I had grown used to the old clunker and – after the adventure of that first ride over to Ely – had learned to handle it quite well.

We rode slowly, side by side, generating a visible trail of dust as we left the paved road and ventured a couple of miles down the series of gravel lanes that served to connect some of the outlying fields that Ned and Mary farmed down by the river.

"Ned, Charlie, and Ned's man Frank are out working over toward Freckenham this afternoon, and it's going to be a late one," Jennifer smiled. "So, we have my favorite place all to ourselves.

Besides, the planting here is all late rye, and no-one's going to be interested for about another month or so."

She looked quite pleased with herself, like she had carefully planned the adventure well in advance.

"I think Charlie quite enjoys the farming life," I observed. "It's like he was made to be out in the fields with Ned." I grinned in Jennifer's direction and she returned the gesture with a broad smile.

Most of the fields, from the smallest half-acre plot to the big twenty and even fifty acre tracts we would soon be harvesting for wheat, are enclosed by tight hedgerows, accessible through breaks or gates in the corners. Occasionally there would be a tall row of trees, planted in a line between the adjacent fields to act as wind breaks. Over time, the countryside had taken on the appearance of one enormous maze.

After a while the road we were following gave out, and we had to ride through a series of fields, gates, and tracks. Eventually we worked our way beyond a small gap in one of the hedgerows; it opened up to a grassy slope running gently down to a small river.

The area was sheltered on three sides by the tall vegetation, and across the river a thick stand of willow trees came down to the water. In both directions tight bends isolated this section of the river. A massive oak tree grew out of one of the hedges, spreading its thick limbs well over the water, where a deep pool reflected the trees on the other side and a spattering of blue sky above. Speckled sunshine made its way through to the soft grass, and the quiet water danced in the early afternoon light.

"None of the property around here is worked except for Ned's rye field behind us," Jennifer explained. "It's all grown over and has been for years. I've been coming down here since I was about eight years old. To read, think, and sometimes wiggle my toes in the water."

She dumped her bag and spread a light blanket on the grass. "Here, let's pull out the picnic stuff." The grass was soft, springy, and mossy - it made a perfect place to relax.

Jennifer had prepared a classic "Plowman's Lunch." She unwrapped a cloth containing a small loaf of bread, two enormous hunks of cheese, a couple of rosy apples, a big slice of meat pie, and a flask of hot, sweet, tea. Out there, sitting cross-legged across the blanket from the most beautiful hazel-eyed girl in the whole world, enjoying the sultry warmth of a clear summer's day in the countryside, nothing could have tasted better.

We laughed, taking it in turns to tell corny jokes. We were serious too, as we talked about our fears regarding the war. And we were also full of hope, young and optimistic despite the conflict, enjoying the beautiful day.

"When do you think you'll see your mum and dad again?" I asked as we cleaned away the crumbs and pulled out our books to read away the afternoon. "They sound so cool and I really want to meet them."

"Well, my mum gets enough leave to make the trip up here to see us at the end of the month…"

"I know you can't wait."

"… But, they really can't give Dad more than a day here and there because there just aren't enough qualified pilots, and the German planes keep coming and coming."

"Are you worried about him?"

"Not really." Her eyes sparkled as she warmed to the subject of her dad. "You should see him in a Spitfire. He can fly circles around anyone, and when he's not flying missions he's training other guys.

"One day, just before the war, I watched him set down a plane with half a working engine and an undercarriage that was stuck in the wrong position. He dropped it on the runway soft as a feather. They still talk about the emergency landing he executed directly on a cricket pitch during the middle of a game. Legend has it he jumped out and asked if it was a good time for tea, and if not could they direct him to the closest pub!"

I listened admiringly. I could just picture the scene.

"My dad has more style than anyone I know, Henry," Jennifer said. "And I don't believe the Luftwaffe could touch him even if it was ten to one."

The passion just poured out of her.

"What about you?" she asked. "How about your mum, or even your dad?"

"Mum would probably love to come to Isleham for a visit - although I'm not sure she could get dad to cooperate. But for him to make the journey all the way here? Good grief, it would take some kind of a miracle."

After a while we settled into our books. It was cozy and warm, and we had enjoyed a good lunch, so without meaning to I fell sound asleep. I'm not sure how long I was snoozing, but I woke up to find Jennifer tickling my nose with the end of a long piece of grass.

"Hey, Henry," she said. "Want to go for a swim?"

The air was still, and the day had turned hot. There were small beads of perspiration standing out on her arms and face. The soft skin above her lip sparkled with moisture. It certainly sounded like a good idea.

"Where?"

"The river is sandy, and great for splashing. Plus the hole drops down five or six feet and there's just enough room for a couple of strokes. Or, if you're adventurous, jumping in from up in the tree."

"Aren't you forgetting swimsuits?" I laughed nervously.

Jennifer smiled wryly. "Hey, this is the queen of skinny dipping you're talking to here!"

I must have turned visibly white. I know I caught my breath. "I'd do it, you know," she said wickedly. And I didn't doubt for a moment that she would. "But don't worry, Henry. For you I'm willing to involve underwear."

I swallowed hard, but still must have looked completely shocked, because Jennifer laughed again with that playful, *Devil may care* attitude of hers. Then she smacked me with one of the towels she had pulled out of her bag.

"I'm wearing plain white undies and a sleeveless cotton T-shirt, Henry. Come on! I'm as innocent as a nun. Besides, it'll be fun."

I wasn't so sure about the nun part, but I did remember how natural and easygoing she had been, sprawling around on the grass that first walk we took together. Then there was that letter she had read from her dad, and the way she had thrown the towel at me when I got home from Ely, soaked to the skin from the rain.

Jennifer obviously had a different way of looking at things than the average sixteen-year-old girl. She wasn't about to get all bashful and modest with me. So I decided that if she was relaxed and at ease, then there wasn't any point in my stressing out enough for the both of us.

She unbuttoned the oversized shirt she was wearing, slipping it off her shoulders as I involuntarily held my breath. She was right, the demure, sleeveless, V-neck "T" she had on underneath was not much different from something any girl might have worn to play tennis.

"Go ahead, Henry," she said, "your turn."

Well here goes nothing, I thought, and pulled my T-shirt over my head. After several weeks of Saturdays and afternoons helping Ned and Charlie in the fields, I was sporting a decent tan for the first time in my life. I felt quite proud of myself.

Then she kicked her shoes off, and I followed suit, carefully stuffing my socks inside each other and rolling them up with my shirt.

Jennifer didn't even stop to look around, hide behind a tree, or make sure that the coast was clear. She just looked at me, smiled, and pulled her skirt down over her knees before throwing it in an untidy heap on the blanket.

I don't know how she had managed it, but she was tanned all the way up. I tried not to stare at her legs, but they were spectacular. Somewhat of a tomboy, she was well toned with a trim figure. She smiled again, and then raised her eyebrows in an unspoken question.

So I unzipped my trousers and tried to pull them off casually, with as little self-consciousness as possible, like I did this kind of thing every day. I folded them carefully, and we stood there for a moment, down to our briefs, just looking at each other.

Suddenly, she made a move for the tree. "Personally, I like to get the cold splash over with quickly," she said, "so I always use the direct approach."

Jennifer was all about the direct approach, no question. And I watched, openmouthed, as the first girl I had ever seen in her skivvies shimmied up the enormous oak tree and perched on the middle of a thick limb that hung about six feet over the dark pool at the bend in the river.

"Bombs away!" she yelled, and entered the water feet first, before surfacing and shaking her head in the sunlight. "Come on in," she laughed. "You can't stand around in your underwear all day!"

So I climbed out on the bough, paused on the long sturdy branch for a second, and then plunged into the cool water. After the initial shock it was extremely refreshing, and we were soon splashing and laughing together as if this was the kind of thing we did together all the time.

We must have played around in the water for close to an hour, running out and jumping back in, climbing the tree, and swimming around, all without the slightest awareness of each other beyond the simple fun of companionship. Then we remembered the apples we had saved for later, and I climbed out of the water once again to retrieve them.

As I sauntered back down the grassy bank, Jennifer eased out of the deep water to join me by the edge. The sun, changing its angle ever so slightly, bounced off her hair to produce a kind of halo effect. The moment caught me off guard.

"Stop right there," I said. She was a vision.

And she did. In that instant, soaked through and disheveled from an hour in the water, I realized that white cotton, no matter how carefully manufactured, appears essentially transparent when it gets sopping wet. Not only that, it conforms to the body like a second skin. Jennifer had nothing on under that sleeveless shirt, and the sunlight caught her just so, as if to add its own exclamation to my observation.

"Mr. Bradley," she said softly, understanding the substance of my gaze, "I do believe you are taking advantage of this situation."

"But you are so unreasonably beautiful," I confessed. "I hope that doesn't sound corny?"

"Not at all," she smiled. "But I do think we'd better get dressed."

I turned around to get the towels.

"Wait one moment," Jennifer said, stepping toward me.

"What?" I replied, turning back around.

She was right there, having moved directly in front of me. And, as I turned, she cupped one hand behind my head and kissed me, full on the lips, the inside of her wet knee just touching the outside of mine, her other hand resting on my chest.

She tasted wet, cool, delicious, and indescribably fresh. The kiss lasted the best part of two long seconds. It left me breathless.

"There," she said. "I couldn't help myself."

Quickly, I threw her one of the apples, and we munched on them while doing our best to towel off before pulling on the rest of our clothes.

Originally, it had been our intention to let our "swimwear" dry on our bodies in the warm air, while we lounged around some more and maybe poured another cup of tea. But we both realized how dangerous that might have been.

I suspect that Jennifer was quite comfortable with a little danger – or a lot. But we both realized I needed a little less of that kind of heat. At least for that particular day.

Derek Maul

CHAPTER TWENTY-THREE

A Short Lesson in Cricket

That week it took all the strong will and self-discipline I had to resist sharing the details of our afternoon at the river. All I said to Charlie was, "Jennifer took me out for a picnic, and we had a great time. I really, really, really think that I like her a lot."

Charlie had nodded, smiled, and shifted the conversation immediately back to Friday afternoon's upcoming cricket match. The game was all most of the boys really cared about that week. It was the annual contest between the Newmarket boys' team and a stuck-up private academy located on the other side of the town. The two schools had apparently developed a rather intense rivalry over the years, and it was going to be the first time in a decade the game had been scheduled out at the exclusive academy.

Charlie, who loved sports statistics of every kind, had signed on to assist our team's official scorekeeper, and I had been fortunate enough to be invited to join the playing squad. I had always batted number three in Folkestone (for American readers, this is like batting "cleanup" in baseball), and had – at times - enjoyed considerable success.

The morning and afternoon school schedule switch had made it impossible for me to stay in my home school lineup. In consequence, arrangements were made for my eligibility to transfer to the local Newmarket team, in order to align with the reversed academic timetable.

A few of the teachers owned cars and between them they had enough room to transport the team to Charter Academy. We made our way across town in a motley caravan of dilapidated vehicles. As soon as we turned into Charter's main driveway from the Newmarket road, I realized this was going to be no ordinary school cricket match.

First we drove through the impressive set of enormous wrought iron gates. The gates (which I'm sure would eventually be requisitioned as a contribution to a wartime metal drive) were only one part of an imposing entry that also featured the school crest set in burnished bronze. We found ourselves traversing a long, curved drive lined with stately elm trees. Either side of the broad avenue, acres of beautifully maintained playing fields provided a lush vista. Beyond the fields there were deep woods to one side, and an expansive lake on the other.

After a good half mile, the drive swept in front of the stately mansion that had been converted into the exclusive preparatory school. We pulled up in a ragged line and all tumbled out, presenting a scruffy looking crew. A welcoming committee stood on the front steps, looking down their noses at us and trying to add a sense of formality to the occasion.

One of the older boys stepped forward and introduced himself to Mr. Philpot, our games master.

"I say old chap" – he was an excessively pale young man, wearing one of those straw "boater" hats you often see rich people wearing as they float lazily down the River Thames in a royal barge – "You must be Philpot. My name is Dickie Adams. Smashing to meet you."

Mr. Philpot was a tough but fair teacher who never took even the slightest hint of disrespect from anyone. He admired hard work, bristled at injustice, and couldn't stand even an insinuation of snobbery.

I could see Mr. Philpot wrestling with a decision regarding how to respond, and I swear I saw his lips move as he counted to ten not once but twice, before electing to let it go. He must have decided taking the boy down a peg or two simply wasn't worth the effort. So he let the young toff's condescending air and lack of manners roll right off his back. Our teacher shook the extended hand politely.

"Glad to be here," he managed, his neck turning beet red as he swallowed hard.

"Right you are," the pasty teen continued. "If you'll just follow Monroe and Saunders here, they'll show you where you can get changed into your cricket togs."

We followed Monroe and Saunders, all the way around to the back of the main building, where we were amazed to behold a series of wide brick terraces set in front of the longest row of French doors I have ever seen.

"That would be our dining room," Saunders pointed out when he caught me ogling.

A flight of stone steps at least fifty feet wide swept off the terraces and down to the immaculately prepared cricket field.

It was the most beautiful manicured grass I had ever seen in my life. The field had been mowed – and rolled - that morning, in a crisscross pattern that left a gorgeous checkered effect on the turf. In the middle, the twenty-two yard by ten foot pitch was cut and rolled closer than the Center Court at Wimbledon or the greens at St. Andrew's. Around the boundary, a clean white rope marked the edge of the playing area, and a large, fancy scoreboard completed the ensemble of state-of-the-art facilities.

If all that was not enough to make our mouths drop open, there were three enormous red and white striped tents pitched around the perimeter. In the tents I could see tables of sandwiches, meat pies, strawberries and cream, and other delectable treats set out, while scores of straw-boatered boys milled around in their white pants and navy-blue jackets.

"If there's a war on," observed Charlie as he looked around at all the luxury and the extravagance, "then I don't think the people here know anything about it!"

"Look," one of our friends stammered, hardly able to contain himself, "there's a whole tent just for tea."

Of course we weren't going there just yet, but we did find ourselves already looking forward to the late-afternoon break. For now we were led around to the far side of the field – laid out in an elongated oval – where a handsome wooden building labelled, "Visitors' Pavilion" housed our comfortable changing facilities.

"Boys," Mr. Philpot stage-whispered to us as we stood outside gawking, "we're going to go on in now, then I want you to spend a few minutes pretending that we have nice cricket uniforms to change into!"

We went in, took our school uniform blazers off - ties too - and rolled our shirt sleeves up to the elbow. A few of the boys had canvas athletic footwear to exchange their shoes for, and we set our equipment (batting pads, bats, wicket-keeper's gloves, and a few well-worn cricket balls) out by the row of comfortable lawn chairs set up in front of our pavilion.

A little while later, after a cue from Mr. Philpot, we emerged onto the field, warming up with a little throwing and catching. After a few more minutes Mr. Philpot beckoned Keith Parcells, the team captain, and they walked to the center of the field, where the umpires waited, to chat with the opposing skipper and take the coin toss.

Keith walked back rather stiffly, fairly bristling. He called the team together. His face was crimson and he clenched both fists tightly.

"Right then," he blurted a little too loudly. "Who wants to kick a little snotty-nosed arse?"

"Eh... what happened?"

"First, the arrogant snot wanted to know if we'd ever played 'real competitive cricket' before. He smirked and said something about how they'd be happy to give us twenty runs to help get us started. Then he wanted to know if we needed to borrow any decent equipment. He said his dad was always happy to lend a hand to help out the 'poor boys from the town'."

Keith shook his head in disgust. "I was about to recommend the family proctologist when Mr. Philpot gave me the eye. Then he told us to toss the coin and get on with it. So anyway, that's the scoop. They bat first, and we probably get to go in sometime after tea."

*   *   *   *

Cricket – especially for those unfamiliar with the ins and outs of the game – is a unique sporting event. It's played with a solid red ball featuring a raised, stitched seam. It's as hard as a baseball, yet no one wears gloves except for the wicket-keeper (cricket's equivalent to the catcher in baseball).

Cricket bats have long, thick, flat wooden blades. The stumps (three two-foot tall vertical sticks) define the strike zone as from mid-thigh all the way to the ground. Two "bails" are balanced on top of the stumps, designed to detect even the slightest contact from the ball by means of falling to the ground.

The fielding side takes all eleven players onto the field, and the opposing team sends in two batsmen at any given time.

There are two wickets (sets of stumps and bails), one each end of the pitch, and each time the batters cross, making it safely to the opposite end (twenty-two yards), a run is scored – or two… or three… if there's time to cross again. If the ball is hit out of bounds on the fly – called "hitting a six" - the value is six runs. If the ball is hit out of bounds having bounced or rolled - "hitting a four" - four runs are scored. With the pitch situated in the middle of the field of play, the ball can be hit, or redirected, any direction, over all three-hundred sixty degrees.

An "out" occurs when:

a) The wicket is hit by the pitch with sufficient force to dislodge the bails from the stumps. The ball is "bowled" straight arm, typically bouncing once before reaching the batter.
b) A ball is caught on the fly after it is hit.
c) The runner is thrown out while running the length between the wickets.
d) A ball that otherwise would have hit the wicket is obstructed by the batter's leg ("LBW" or *leg before wicket*).

When the ball is bowled, the batter is under no obligation to run once the ball is struck (this lack of purposeful action can sometimes become tiresome). The wicket can simply be protected with a defensive block. Or, if the ball is obviously going to miss, it can be ignored altogether. The decision to run is based on the likelihood of successfully reaching the other end. Consequently, a skillful and careful batter can stay at his post for a long "at bat." Time, though, is often at a premium, and runs do eventually need to be scored. Therefore, strategy often demands that risks are taken.

After the ball has been bowled six times (one "over"), the fielding team reconfigures, and another bowler takes a turn from the other end of the pitch. Thereafter, "overs" alternate from each end throughout the game.

An inning is complete either when ten batters have been retired, or the team has posted enough runs to safely "declare" their inning over. An early declaration is a strategic move utilized to make sure enough time remains to win the game.

Such a game could have three possible outcomes:

1) The second team scores more runs than the first team.
2) The first team retires the second team before they equal or beat their first inning score.
3) Darkness falls before the second team is retired, even though they don't have enough runs. In such a case a draw is declared.

(In the modern era, most schools play "limited over" games, where each team faces an equal number of balls. The winner is – simply - the team posting the highest score.)

*   *   *   *

At Charter Academy our casually attired team took the field to a smattering of quiet applause, emerging from the deck chairs and tents of our privileged hosts. The first two Charter Academy batsmen walked out to an enthusiastic reception. Both boys were decked in pure white flannels. They wore caps sporting the school colors, their white leather shoes were specifically designed for cricket, and they modeled sleeveless white sweaters with the school insignia sewn over the breast.

It was exactly two o'clock when the game started. We could be assured of good light until around 8:40 in the evening, after taking a twenty-minute break for "tea" a little before 5:00.

It was slow going from the first ball, and Charter Academy had trouble putting runs on the board. Their number three batter stuck in there, however, hitting a "six" and three "4's" on the way to a respectable thirty-eight. But by four o'clock the home team still had less than a hundred runs, with seven men down. That's when they decided to play defensively and do their best to run down the clock so there would be insufficient time for our team to score enough runs to win.

When the umpire looked at his watch and called for tea it was 4:45. Charter had scored one hundred twelve runs, and there were still only eight men out. If we were to stand any chance of winning, we had to dismiss two more batters in a hurry, giving ourselves time to score some quick runs before dark.

Tea was set up on folding tables at the perimeter. In that glorious fifteen minutes I drank three cups and helped myself to two chocolate eclairs plus a cream horn, as well as an enormous piece of fruit cake I covertly stuffed in my pocket on my way back out to the field.

The tea interval must have invigorated Charter's team, because the last batters put another thirty runs on the board between them.

By the time we got the tenth man out, around thirty minutes beyond our comfort zone, we were looking at one hundred forty-three runs needed to win. There was still a lot of cricket to play, and it was only a few minutes before six o'clock.

My turn came along with a little more than one hour and fifteen minutes remaining. I was in the batting order at number seven. It was a dicey situation at that point because, after a miserable hour and fifteen minutes, five of our best batters had been dismissed, with only fifty-two runs posted. Knowing my reputation as a slugger, with the potential to either score big or get myself out quickly, Mr. Philpot took me aside.

"What do you think, Henry? I'd hate to go home without beating these toffy-nosed twerps! We can either batten down the hatches, and hold on for a draw, or we can make an honest run at them. I hate settling for a tie, but the real question is going to be, 'Can you see the ball clearly, or not?' You'll know after the bowler sends the first couple your way."

I appreciated the way Mr. Philpot phrased his question. He wasn't commenting on the state of the light – it would be good for well over another hour. He was asking me to let him know if I was "in the zone" or not.

"You know me sir," I said. "It's never any fun to play for a draw."

"Then it's up to you, Henry. If you want to go for it, I'm giving you the green light."

I loved getting the green light! However, I had also built my dubious reputation by going after a lot of balls I really couldn't hit. I needed to be "on" today, or I was going to end up letting everyone down.

So I made my way out to the pristine pitch quickly, punched the other batsman in the arm enthusiastically, dug in, and got set carefully for the first ball. The smell of the grass, the weight of the bat in my hands, the aroma of the freshly applied linseed oil on the aged wood, and the golden glow of the evening sun all worked together to create a magical moment.

Could I see clearly enough to make a difference? Well, the answer to that question came as plain as a revelation, at the precise moment the bowler hit "the crease" and the ball began to emerge from his hand at the top of the long arc.

His arm came around, the ball came into clear focus, and it was as if everything retreated into frame-by-frame slow motion. I could see the stitching on the bright red ball. I could almost read the name of the manufacturer. I could distinctly pick out the direction of the spin.

I understand that – typically – it's a smart move to take that first ball in a defensive posture, waiting to get a feel for what kind of stuff the bowler has to offer. But instead, I stepped forward as the ball left his hand, planted my left foot firmly in the grass, and swung with the sure and certain knowledge that I would make solid contact. I smacked the ball cleanly on the half-volley, a split instant after it bounced on the pristine turf. My hit made the gratifying sound that comes from the sweet spot, and the bright red cricket ball sailed over the unfortunate bowler's head and beyond two more players before passing the boundary on the fly and careening into a row of lawn chairs in the distance.

The umpire put both hands in the air to indicate a "six." It was as solid a strike as I have ever launched in my life.

After that it was just a matter of the other boys holding their ground.

Sometime around eight-twenty, with the score still in the host team's favor at one hundred-forty-two to one hundred forty, and with the solid cushion of two outs between us and defeat, I waved my bat decisively at one more ball. The unimpressive delivery slotted conveniently into the groove I had worked all evening, and I cracked my fifth "six" of the day, directly into the disappointed Charter Academy crowd gathered in front of the home pavilion.

Combined with a healthy smattering of "fours," "two's," and "singles," I finished up with a satisfying eighty-two run contribution to a decisive – and enthusiastically celebrated - Newmarket victory.

*   *   *   *

That evening I took a late walk with Jennifer and Newton, basking in the glow of the day's events, still relishing the memory of our long Monday afternoon picnic. We held hands, walking slowly through the pitch blackness to the park.

"Why haven't you kissed me since Monday afternoon?" Jennifer asked.

"I still haven't gotten over that one," I laughed. "I can still feel it all the way down to my toes."

We continued walking as we talked, and I luxuriated in the ease of our conversation, the closeness I felt through her hand, and the instinctive openness that flowed back and forth between us.

"To be honest," I continued, "I'm scared of breaking the spell. I'm not superstitious or anything, but my life has been too perfect this week. My birthday was the best. Plus I got that letter from my dad, and it has made me start to rethink everything."

I stopped and turned to look directly at her. "Then the Monday picnic with you was unbelievable. It's been a good week at school too, and this evening's fun on the cricket field just topped it all off."

I couldn't help but notice how warm and soft her hand felt in mine.

"I've thought about kissing you all week, Jennifer," I said, carefully. "But I'm scared something will come up that will spoil everything that's already happened. I don't want this war messing with my life anymore. I like my life just like it is. I don't want to burst this beautiful bubble I'm in right now, and I'm nervous that anything I do might change what's turned out to be the very best week ever of my entire life."

"So what if the bubble bursts, evacuee?" she answered softly. "What if you had lost the game today, instead of winning? What if we had a bad argument? What if something made us all suddenly remember we really are in a terrible war? What if you had to go home tomorrow?"

Jennifer looked up into the sky and gestured to the stars. She smiled gently. "Would all the goodness, and beauty, and light that life is all of a sudden be any different?"

CHAPTER TWENTY-FOUR

Suddenly the Light was Gone

Sometimes, without knowing anything at all, you suddenly know everything. Sometimes, absolutely nothing that happens is surprising, even if it turns out to be the least likely thing in the world. Sometimes, it is as if the entire emotional spectrum of a thing comes in and starts to take effect before even the event itself. One day late in July, just the day after the cricket game at Charter Academy, one hot and sultry summer's evening, less than twenty-four hours after Jennifer had asked me, "What if?" this was exactly what happened.

Charlie and I had been working out in the fields all Saturday afternoon with Ned, throwing baled hay up onto the truck bed. Stacking and heaving. It was back-breaking work. Ned handled the bundles with a pitchfork, the bales sailing easily over his shoulder and up where they belonged. Charlie and I alternated stacking and driving the tractor.

There was dust, more dust, and scratchy straw that worked its way into everywhere. Impossibly small flies, attracted by our sweat, came in swarms. Our mouths were full, it seemed, of powdered summer farm. Eventually, as the sun finally began to diminish, late into the hot evening, Ned at last said, "Enough," and we struck out walking the half mile or so toward home.

The feeling hit me just as soon as we left the field, hard. It was almost as if I had been punched in the stomach, or smacked in the head. I reeled visibly. I almost stumbled. I put a hand up over my eyes.

Charlie noticed.

"What's up? Work too hard or something?"

"I don't know. Everything just feels wrong, like my balance is off, like something bad has happened. Whatever it is, it's not right, but I don't know what. I don't understand it, Charlie, but I've felt like something was coming on all afternoon."

"Beats me," Charlie said. "Maybe you're getting a summer cold?" Then he started to make some corny joke about my mental stability, but thought better of it and stopped himself. He obviously sensed that this was real – whatever it was.

We walked silently down East Fen Road back toward the cottage. I felt worse and worse the closer we got. It was a black night, and there wasn't any comfort in the sky.

"Good night, Henry." Charlie peeled off at Ned and Mary's place.

"See ya."

I felt a horrible emptiness in the pit of my stomach. I looked over my shoulder to yell for my friend to come back, to walk with me, but he had trotted up the driveway too quickly, and was already closing the door, surrounded by bouncing dogs.

Ahead, the increasingly dim outline of Lily's cottage merged into the soupy darkness of wartime blackout, the pale evening light now almost completely gone. By the time I walked up to the door I was cold, clutching myself to stay warm. I was scared too, nervous, and ready to run for my life at the first sign of a threat. I had no idea what this feeling meant, but my guard was up and I was in a defensive, fight of flee, mode. The whole world was deathly quiet, not a hint of light showed through the dark curtains. I paused outside, rooted to my spot in the driveway, too unnerved to open the door.

As I hesitated in front of the entry, unsure of my emotions, uncertain how to proceed, I heard the ring-ringing of a bicycle bell as Jennifer swung into the driveway. I turned toward her, anxious for a dose of her natural ebullience.

"What are you standing around for?" she called out in her jaunty voice. "Let's go inside and I'll see what we can round up for supper. I don't know about you, but I'm half starved."

She pecked me on the cheek easily, as if we were some kind of official item. As she hustled me in I felt some momentary relief from my apprehension. But I was still extremely nervous, anxious, and afraid.

Jennifer stood in front of me and took my hand. "Your skin is all clammy. You look like you've seen a ghost, Henry."

That was exactly how I felt.

"Here," she continued, walking over to the counter that collected all the household debris, "there was something from your mum in today's mail."

She tossed a thick envelope my way and bounced into the kitchen to put the kettle on the stove.

The moment the travel-worn manila envelope landed in my hands I knew that it contained bad news. Don't ask me how, but all the forbidding feelings of the past half-hour seemed to come into focus, centered on the letter from my home town. I held it cautiously and shuffled to the living room sofa where the cat, maybe sensitive to my mounting distress, jumped immediately into my lap and began to rub my hand with the side of her face.

I took a deep breath, slid my pocket knife between the folds of the envelope, and yanked out the carefully folded letter. As I did, a newspaper clipping fell into my lap. I stared at the section of newsprint for a moment before setting the letter aside and picking up the article. It was dated Wednesday, July twenty-fourth. A small headline was circled: "Teenager Dies in Worst Local Shelling of War." I paused, took another deep breath, and read on:

> Yesterday evening more than twenty large caliber German shells found targets in the Folkestone area. While several local businesses evidently sustained major damage, it was the death of sixteen-year-old Graham Fern that marked the attack as tragic. Graham was assisting his father, Mr. Gary Fern, with an automobile repair. Mr. Fern escaped injury in the incident. Funeral services will be held Saturday, noon, at Folkestone Baptist Church.

The world around me seemed to stand still. The space my soul inhabits effectively imploded, and my heart collapsed like a deck of cards. I heard this shrill and deeply disturbed rushing sound trigger inside of my head. It became louder and louder.

"No!" A voice, mine, faint at first, fought against the harsh, conflicting noise.

"No!" Louder still.

"No!" And I couldn't even seem to hear or understand myself think. I grabbed the letter, bunching it up in my hand. The clipping dropped to the floor as I blundered my out into the dark night, ignoring the pale, distant voice that was Jennifer asking me something I couldn't really hear.

I didn't pause, I didn't look around, I just moved. As soon as I was clear of the house I turned right and ran, heading down East Fen Road as far and as long as I could. Numb, angry, wounded, insensible, oblivious. I don't remember much detail except later, much later, turning around and making my way back, walking slowly. I ended up, for some reason that wasn't clear to me at the time, at the old parish church in the center of the village. The ancient front door was unlocked so I eased my way in, going all the way to the front, crying silently in the second pew for God knows how long, deep into the long night.

And that was where they found me - Charlie, actually. I sat hunched over, still clutching the partially read piece of mail. I recognized my friend's footsteps as he came down the aisle, knelt on the pew in front, and looked over at me with deep sadness etched in his face.

"We've been looking for you all night, Henry."

"Why?" I said, uncooperatively.

"Saw the clipping. You dropped it at Lily's."

"Then you know."

"Right."

I punched him on the arm, hard, frustration and pain dripping out of every pore. I wanted to break something. I wanted to run again. I wanted to scream. I wanted to throw something through a stained-glass window. I wanted to cry some more. I didn't know what I wanted.

"The funeral was today, Charlie. We should have been there."

"I know," he nodded.

"I loved him too, you know," Charlie whispered, his eyes full with tears.

So we sat there, a few inches apart but very much together. Crying silently. Pain etched into our faces. Sorrow dripping from every pore. Less angry now, and more sad. Waiting to understand.

And then a most marvelous thing happened. Charlie dug around in his pocket and pulled out a small box of matches. Next, he walked up to the table at the top of the worn steps, where he lit one of the candles, just one. But that one candle was enough to fill the entire front of the stone church with enough yellow light to reveal the details that marked the sanctuary as a place of worship.

Charlie came back to my pew, tugged on my sleeve, and led me back to the steps. We knelt there together.

"Lord God," he began, "we want to remember Graham. Graham was our really good friend. We feel awful about what happened, and we just want you to know about it. Please help his mum and dad as they try to deal with this, too. Thank you. Amen."

Then he dug me in the ribs. I didn't know what to do. I didn't know what to say, or how to say it. I just didn't know. I've never been very good at praying with words.

But then it came to me. *"The Lord is mine... the... my... Shepherd,"* I tripped over the words, *"I shall... I shall not want..."* And – as I went along, haltingly - I realized that I was remembering every word of the Twenty-third Psalm.

Charlie joined in, and we stumbled along together, tears streaming down our faces, more confident as we went deeper into the psalm. And as we reached the part, *"Yea, though I walk through the valley of the shadow of death, I will fear no evil: for thou art with me; thy rod and thy staff they comfort me,"* it seemed like there were other voices too.

And, sure enough, I felt hands placed on our shoulders, and the voices blended. My voice, Charlie's voice, and Lily's. Ned, Mary, and Jennifer too.

"Surely goodness and mercy shall follow me all the days of my life," we all said, with a little more strength now, *"and I will dwell in the house of the Lord forever."*

And I just knelt there, my mother's letter still crumpled in my hand, for what seemed a long time, until my eyes at last cleared - just a little, and Lily finally said, "Let's go on home."

We walked home slowly, Jennifer's hand in mine, through the dark middle of a dark night. I kept seeing our sunny hilltop perch above Folkestone, overlooking the English Channel, Graham Fern sitting there with yet another piece of half chewed grass hanging from his mouth.

"Mr. Hitler had better watch out for us if he wants to try anything with England any time soon!" he was saying.

"You tell him, Graham," I said aloud, "you tell him."

I SLEHAM - 1990

Henry didn't quite know what to expect from Isleham. He and Elizabeth had taken the bus from Ely, and it had been another spur of the moment decision, following the story a little farther down the trail. The bus was a rickety vehicle that looked and felt decidedly 1940's. After they arrived they walked around the village for an hour. Henry pointed out the most important landmarks, while Elizabeth asked questions and took photos.

"It's a peculiar thing," Henry said as they sat on a park bench looking toward the old parish church, "but it goes back to the experience Charlie and I had over in Ely Cathedral, when we were overwhelmed by the effect of the architecture and the light. That's what led me to seek refuge here that night, after I read the newspaper clipping and found out about Graham."

"But this church is nowhere near as grand or imposing," Elizabeth pointed out. "It's not even somewhere you even went to on a Sunday morning."

"I know," Henry said. "But I've been thinking about it a lot, and I'm pretty sure I understand what happened here. That moment, when everyone showed up and we kind of fell into saying *The Lord is my Shepherd* together - is essentially the same as what happened when we rode over to Ely. It was the same thing we experienced when we were blown away by the architecture."

"You're going to have to explain," Elizabeth turned in the bench and sat sideways to pay closer attention.

"I'm one hundred percent sure the common denominator was – is - faith," Henry said. "You felt it in Ely too, didn't you? Even though you said you're not a go-to-church person at all. But it's more than that. I think there's something deep and rooted and true that tugs at us when our defenses are down, and it's harder to pretend it's not there at some times than it is at others."

Henry's sincerity was obvious, but Elizabeth felt she had to ask just the same. "You're not trying to push religion on me, are you?"

"That's not a game I know how to play," he smiled. "I just know I haven't had to go through any of this alone, not once, not ever. Not when my friend Graham died. Not when my dad passed away, or my mum. Not even when I lost Deborah just a few months ago...."

Elizabeth took Henry's hand and squeezed it. The early evening light caught the edges of the church, and a gentle breeze stirred the leaves of the old chestnut trees. Elizabeth felt she was on the edge of something important.

"You are one more complicated story," she said.

"I've heard that before," he laughed. "How about we get some fish and chips, and then find a couple of rooms at a B&B? I think we might be able to wrap up the story this evening over a couple of pots of tea."

CHAPTER TWENTY-FIVE - 1940

A Long Walk for the Long View

Steve and I moped around for a couple of days, feeling sorry for ourselves, sniffling occasionally, and drinking lots of tea. Lily was especially solicitous, fussing over us like a pair of wounded puppies. Even the taciturn Ned came across as the warm, caring man he really was on the inside, his routinely disinterested mannerisms sidelined - slightly - to provide glimpses of tenderness we never knew were possible. Overall, we felt cared for, and that was good.

At school I thought about Trevor, the kid from Liverpool who had lost his father at sea, and who we had all let down so badly. I thought about how he had tried so desperately to reach out to the rest of us. But we're all different, and I did not want to connect – not with anyone. Consequently I brushed off supportive comments and told other kids who wanted to make us feel better to go take a hike.

Charlie and I understood what we had lost, we understood each other, and we could be supportive – we felt – by just being miserable together. Maybe we would actually talk about it later.

Then I thought about Abraham, the international student who was a refugee from Hitler's terror campaign in Austria. There he was, at school every day, having gone through the worst thing imaginable, still wondering if the rest of his family would even make it out. Chances were they would end up in one of the concentration camps we were just beginning to hear smatterings of information about. Yet Abraham was always so positive, so willing to talk about the situation in his homeland. Somehow he seemed to believe that his life was not defined by the horror of this tragedy. But I did not want to talk with him, either.

Instead I felt an overpowering emptiness slipping over me like an envelope. The light really was gone, and the effect was increasingly claustrophobic.

I guess I approached things differently than Charlie. He loved Graham too, I knew that, but his feelings were always more tidily dealt with, it seemed, and he went on about the rest of his life more easily. Charlie was about done with abject misery within a day or two, and he seemed to slump along gloomily out of solidarity with me. He may well have been in pain, but I could tell he was ready to get on with things. I didn't exactly resent him for it, but I couldn't come close at all to getting on.

As for me, I woke up every morning feeling that the world was no longer the same place that it had been, that it would never be so bright, so good, so light, so alive. Even though I hadn't seen my friend in a couple of months, I felt his death profoundly. We were The Three: Graham, Henry, and Charlie - always in that order. To tell the truth, I felt at least one third dead.

The sense of emptiness seemed to be exacerbated with each new day. In fact, it felt like it was growing. And I was lonely, too. It was as if the dark cloud that heralded the news of Graham's death was settling in for the long haul, seeping its treacherous way through every chink of armor and into every pore. My head was thick with it, and its weight seemed to actually push down on my shoulders. The movement of my arms and legs also felt restricted, and the sensation settled all the way through to my extremities.

*　　　　　*　　　　　*　　　　　*

It was – I know now - a crushing depression, and by the time the weekend came around I didn't even want to get up. I really couldn't see the point.

Saturday morning Jennifer waltzed in about ten o'clock and threw a pillow at me. Normally the magic light in her eyes would capture me, but not this time.

"Go away," I said, pointedly. It was all I could muster, and she did.

She returned ten minutes later with some tea, adding a warm squeeze of my arm for good measure. But I ignored her, rudely. I ignored the tea too, even though I wanted some, letting the gift stand on the sideboard till it was cold. I emerged only in time for lunch, which I picked at without any real interest before sinking my hands deep in my pockets and slouching back toward my room.

"Not so fast, young man." Lily was standing in my door with a determined look on her face. "Today I'm stripping beds, dusting rooms, washing curtains. I'm starting right here, so you can't go back to bed."

I grimaced, turned without comment, and headed toward the big sofa.

"Not on your life, mister," Lily said. "Just hold it right there for one moment. Spring cleaning is happening all over the entire house this afternoon. And you can't go to Mary's place either," she said, reading my mind.

I felt, and I'm sure I looked, lost. A deep funk of this magnitude needed to be carefully nurtured, and Lily was not cooperating.

"Here's what you're going to do," Lily went on, "and it's not negotiable. It's a nice day outside, and I want you to deliver some things for me to old Mr. Kemp down at The Crossing."

I scowled darkly, and she laughed. "It's either that or dust and wash here with me," Lily explained. "And after that you'll have to run the delivery anyway. Make your choice, then get on with it. What's it going to be?"

"Fine," I muttered. "What do you need me to take?"

"It's all in the small rucksack on my kitchen chair. Thank you, Henry." Then she hurried over to give me a quick squeeze, and she held on for an extra second. It seemed like she was trying her best not to cry.

Outside, it was one of those overcast English summer days that offer a slight breeze and never really try to get too hot. I slung the small pack over my back and started to shuffle down the road, watching my feet as they barely lifted from the gravel, kicking the occasional rock that my toe wouldn't clear.

I was walking because, well, riding my bike would have felt too much like fun – not gloomy enough for me. Besides, how can you shuffle your feet and sulk when you're cruising?

I had two large handkerchiefs stuffed in my pockets because I knew that, sooner or later, I would start to cry. And I did. The strange thing was that I didn't even need to think about Graham - the tears would just come, and with them the darkening black of the cloud that had settled in on my heart and my soul. It gripped me like a vise, squeezing the little light I had in me, tearing me into little pieces.

I felt powerless to do anything about it. Anyway, what did I care? Why should I even try?

Turning off the country road, I followed an even smaller lane past some of the fields we had recently been working in. Fresh cut bales of hay stood in silent rows, waiting to be picked up. Beyond the straggly hedgerows, and a good month or more away from harvest, massive fields of wheat moved like the surface of the ocean in the gentle breeze. I stopped for a moment to lean on a gate, trying to clear my head and to breathe steadily, anything to take away the awful pressure from behind my eyes.

I knew that feeling this way was counterproductive, that it did nothing to serve any positive purpose. I knew that Graham himself would probably think I was being hopelessly melodramatic. But, knowing all that, and then actually having the ability to shake it? Those were two entirely different things.

I felt like a walking advertisement for depression, and I felt powerless, but at the same time I really didn't care. I could feel the ambivalence and the contradictory nature of my emotions. Part of me wanted to cultivate the mood, to luxuriate in the negativity, and to bleed it for all it was worth… And part of me understood that it was worth nothing, and wanted to put it behind me so I could get on with my life.

The dark and moody part, however, was definitely prevailing, winning the tug of war hands down.

Leaning on the gate, fighting the storm clouds in my head, I really didn't see or hear anything else. When I eventually turned around to keep on walking, I was surprised to see Newton sitting in the middle of the lane, waiting patiently for me, his tail thumping the ground as if running into me on the road was the best thing that had ever happened in his life.

"Hi there, boy," I said. "Must be nice to be a dog and not worry about anything else in the world. Did you know there was a war on? Did you know that over in France there are hundreds of thousands of Nazis getting ready to come over here and invade the rest of us? Did you know that they just killed my best friend? Did you know that because of this stupid war I can't even be with my own family?"

Newton just kept on thumping his tail, telling me that the only things that really mattered were me and him, and walking along the lane together, and maybe the occasional rabbit to chase.

"Come on, boy," I called, "let's go."

It must have been a good three miles or more to The Crossing, the point where the quiet lane forded a small river. I have always loved fords. The good ones have been carefully crafted to maintain an even two or three inches of water for the entire crossing. Most fords were constructed with little more width than a single track road, with their edges well marked by stepping stones for the foot traveler. Some of the fancier fords even offered a small wooden footbridge. This particular crossing was less well defined, and grew deep too quickly in rainy weather. The stepping stones were well spaced, but uneven in height, and most people walked right through the middle wearing Wellington boots.

Personally, I was usually a stone hopper, carefully avoiding any unnecessary wetness. While my friends – Graham in particular – were typically inclined to start some kind of tidal wave.

On the far side of the ford there was a rickety wooden gate in the hedgerow. This led down a winding flagstone pathway to Mr.

Kemp's simple two-room cottage. The space between the road and the house was covered in roses, with many of the bushes in full and fragrant bloom.

The Kemps had raised their family here on a small farm. But, for the past few years, since his wife had died, the now-retired Mr. Kemp lived by himself, quiet and content. His two daughters had emigrated to Canada, and he managed to stick it out in the quiet cottage with the help of kind friends, who checked on him every few days and delivered the occasional bag of supplies.

Newton splashed happily across the ford then stood shaking himself on the other side while I picked my way gloomily across the stepping stones. Then, carefully closing the gate behind us, we walked up the path to pull the bell on Mr. Kemp's quaint entry.

After what seemed like an eternity, the old man answered the door. "Good afternoon, Mr. Kemp, My name is Henry Bradley. Lily Duncan asked me to bring you this package."

I fully intended to hand over Lily's package, excuse myself, and walk back the way I had come. Evidently it wasn't going to be that easy.

"Ah, one of the evacuation boys," he said, knowingly, as if my position conferred some kind of a special status. "Please do come in. I need somebody about your height to help me retrieve something from my top cupboard. I've been trying to get at it for most of the week."

*   *   *   *

Arthur Kemp was a handsome gentleman, very striking for his advanced years. Standing about five feet six inches tall, he stood straight as a board and wore a thick thatch of brown hair. A pair of half-rim reading glasses sat perched on the end of his Roman nose, and he wore a stylish tweed sporting jacket that belied his "old age pensioner" status.

"Here we go, young fellow," he said, walking smartly toward the back of the all-in-one kitchen and living room. "Up there, top shelf of the pantry and all the way to the back. It's a box of important Great War paraphernalia I've been meaning to go through all week. You might find you need a chair."

The last thing I wanted to do was to touch anything to do with any war. But Mr. Kemp didn't know a thing about me except the fact that I was an evacuee. Any attempt at an explanation would just complicate things, possibly make me cry, and lead to a bunch of questions I did not want to deal with. So I thought the easiest way out of this would be to get the box down, bid him a good day, and get out of there as fast as I could.

It was actually three large, flat, boxes, tied together with old, yellowed string. Combined, they were about as big as a suitcase, once I retrieved them. Eventually, huffing and puffing a little from the exertion, I got them spread out on the living room table. I stepped back, glanced toward the door, and prepared to take my leave.

"Ah, I understand," Mr. Kemp was regarding me with that evaluative, wise-knowing look that always makes me nervous. "You are young and always in a hurry. Yes?"

I nodded, kind of, and then shook my head unconvincingly. I felt a struggle between my dark mood and sixteen years of well-trained politeness.

"Do me one more small favor, please." The old man looked at me as if trying to decide something. "Let me make you a cup of tea, and offer a piece of cake. It will do you good and – as for me – I don't often get the privilege of receiving guests of your age. Open the boxes, please."

It was a command more than a request, and I sensed a quiet authority in my host. I nodded assent, and he turned up the gas on the kettle, which had been simmering since well before I walked through the door.

Mr. Kemp fussed around in his kitchen, rattling cups and cutting cake, while I carefully removed the lids from the three boxes.

The first box contained nothing but a mountain of papers, tied together in small bundles, with the occasional tattered photograph peeking out. It smelled of dust and mildew. Not anxious to either read anything that old or to pry, I sneezed and moved on to the next package.

Inside box number two sat a partially moth-eaten khaki uniform, folded neatly. Under the uniform I could see a carefully sheathed officer's sword. There were more papers, a small box full of what appeared to be medals, and a dented metal canteen.

I was opening the third box when Mr. Kemp reappeared with a tray containing tea, condiments, and some delicious looking fruit cake.

"And this one," he said, surveying the contents of the last box, "this is the most precious of all."

I sipped the tea – which was very good – and tried to remain disinterested. But there was something compelling about this musty old man and his treasures, and I found myself drawn to him.

"Why is it the most precious?" I asked cautiously, despite myself, trying to maintain my dark mood.

"See." He carefully removed a rounded tin hat with a nasty looking spike on top, a beautifully preserved German Luger handgun, a photograph of a British officer in uniform, and another of two men in civilian clothes with their arms around one another's shoulders, looking directly into the camera.

"This," he said, pointing to the man in uniform, "is James Barrington-Jones. James was my best friend. We fought together in South Africa. You know, the Boer War? Then we were officers together in France. When we were sent to the front in late 1917 we were two of the oldest chaps out there! But things were not going well, and they needed all the experienced officers they could get."

His eyes assumed a faraway look, misting over. And for a moment I thought that I had lost him. "Terrible business," he said, snapping back to 1940, "just terrible." He shook his head slowly.

"Anyway," he continued, his narrative gaining momentum as he went on; "one night, James and I got cut off from our lines in one of those awful raids. You've read your history books, yes? Do you understand about the dynamics of attrition?"

"Yes sir." My history teacher, Mr. Westfall, was fond of telling war stories with as much explicit gory detail as he could get away with. Some parents complained, but the students always loved him.

"Indeed," the old soldier continued. "Several hundred young men would often die for the sake of a hundred yards and a used trench, only to give it up in exchange for a similar amount of death and destruction the very next day."

My host shook his head again, sadly, as if still trying to understand something he knew he never would.

"Where was I? Yes. James and I had both lost our men, and we were trying to work our way back to the British lines. Somewhere in no man's land we got caught in the middle of a terrific bombardment. They used to lay down a literal wall of infernal artillery that moved forward just a few feet every other round or so in order to clear the way for the next raid. We dove for cover, right into an abandoned communications trench that had been dug under the ruins of an old farmhouse."

Mr. Kemp took a deep breath and sipped his tea. I leaned in and waited. It turns out I really was interested after all.

"Well we landed pretty much right on top of two German officers who had found themselves caught in the exact same predicament," he continued with his story. "As you can guess, all hell broke loose for about twenty seconds. It was so dark in there we didn't know what was going on. And then, right at a moment when everything had gone quiet – deathly quiet – a flare or an explosion sent a shaft of light into our ditch, and I could see clearly that James was dead."

He paused for another moment and took a long draft of his tea.

"I could tell it was all over for one of the Germans too, and I had my service revolver leveled right at the head of the other officer. He was desperately trying to unjam his weapon, and was on the point of trying to run me through with his sword." He looked down at the blade I had uncovered in box number two.

"You killed him, right?" I blurted out. Curiosity and excitement – and anger – mixed with my sense of loss and outrage at Graham's death. I was anxious to hear a bloody end to the story.

"I was almost fifty years old," he replied, looking down at the faded photograph of James Barrington-Jones. "I had already seen too much horror and waste. Evidently, so had the German officer. Our eyes met, and in that instant both of us knew that the war was over for us. Over; over in that trench, over on the battle-field, over in the core of who we were as men; over not just for that moment, but forever."

"What happened next?" I gasped, unable to maintain either my sour attitude or the cultivated intention of bitter disinterest.

"I lowered my gun, all the time still looking him in the eye. I flicked on the safety, stuffed the weapon in my pocket, and held out my hand in a gesture of peace.

"'Enough,' I said. "'Enough.' And the German officer replied, knowing just enough English, 'Yes, enough.'"

It has been more than twenty years since that moment, but the old man's eyes filled with tears and his words became quieter the longer he continued his story.

"We shook hands, firmly. And as we did the trench became dark again. We lost eye contact, and we had to rely on trust."

By now I was holding my breath, hanging on to every word.

"The bombardment lasted for close to another hour, the occasional flare offering partial light. And, by the time it was safe enough to return to our respective lines, each with a fallen comrade draped across our shoulders, we had exchanged addresses and sworn that, if we survived, we would look each other up and renew the friendship."

"Well?" I insisted, by this time thoroughly immersed in the story. "How did everything work out?"

"This is Hans," the old man sighed, picking up the second of the photographs, pointing out his friend. "He is godfather to three of my grandchildren. These," he gestured at the box, "are his pistol and his helmet."

"A German? A Hun?"

Mr. Kemp laughed at my expression of wonderment. "No, young man," he said, "a friend, a human being. These Germans are people too. Somewhere in Bavaria my old friend is worrying about me, crying for his country, desperate about his children. I pray for him every night. I pray for them all."

With that he ushered me out of the door, as if – suddenly – he was very tired. And, as Newton and I walked back down the lane, I couldn't get the picture out of my head. They were both Mr. Kemp's best friends. One, Hans, may even be the one who killed the other, James Barrington-Jones. But that wasn't the point, was it?

I was confused, and I didn't know quite how to respond. All I knew was that Mr. Kemp had certainly caused me to start thinking differently, and that much had to be a good thing.

Newton caught back up with me, having given up on the rabbit he had chased across a fallow field. He barked to get my attention.

"Here boy, catch this," I said, throwing a stick for him. He rushed into some tall grass and emerged proudly, carrying the wrong piece of wood. I might have laughed, though I'm not sure. But I did manage to notice that I'd stopped looking exclusively down at my feet.

Derek Maul

CHAPTER TWENTY-SIX

Not Exactly What I'd Expected

The walk back to Isleham was more thoughtful than my mournful plodding on the way out. I didn't know if Lily had deliberately sent me to see Mr. Kemp because she knew he'd tell me his story – I really didn't see how that was possible – or if she had honestly wanted the package delivered, and I just happened to be at the right place at the right time. Or maybe the old soldier told his experiences in The Great War to everyone who came his way?

Had the interaction been providential, had it been accidental, or had it simply been inevitable? Maybe there was no difference between the three? Whatever transpired that day - contrived, destined by the Universe, or quite by chance - I at least had to admit to myself that getting out and doing something active had absolutely been worthwhile. And, even though I wasn't sure if I felt any better regarding the loss of my friend, Graham, I did manage to realize I would much rather go on a long walk than lay around in bed all day.

Newton continued to practice his typical dog routine, which involved variously trotting, circling, and running full speed; he likely covered four times the distance I walked. He rushed ahead, ran back to me instead of waiting, took side deviations in order to chase down more smells, and even attempted to climb the occasional tree as part of his ongoing program of squirrel and bird harassment. Along with all that, Newton still managed to fit in enough time to simply walk by my side, occasionally offering the classic "affirming dog look." His antics positively contributed to the subtle but critically important shift in my mood.

At one point I even stopped for a few minutes to sit on a fence and watch a wheat field move in the wind. It was a peaceful image, set against the vista of blue sky as the clouds began to break up, and the colorful wildflowers that bloomed brightly, massed alongside the hedgerows. I may not have realized it at the time, but all the different elements were beginning to work together to begin to sooth my troubled soul.

About a hundred yards from Lily's house I stopped again, this time leaning on the fence of the pen to watch the pigs. Jennifer was right in there with them, cleaning out the muck and making sure their feed was plentiful. She sported large rubber Wellington boots over her long trousers, and wore an old oversized man's cotton shirt. The afternoon had warmed and she had the sleeves rolled up all the way to her shoulders. Her hair – wayward at the best of times – was held loosely in check by a band, and there was an extra button or two undone below her neck.

She caught me looking.

"Glad to see you out and about, Henry," she said, guardedly. "Do you think maybe you'd like to come out with me for fish and chips later?"

"Only if you take a bath after you've finished playing mud pies with your friends!" I laughed. I had to duck quickly as she sent a handful of something nasty my way at high velocity.

I turned and started to walk toward Lily's cottage, conscious that I was smiling. At the corner, another hundred yards or so beyond home, a green Cambridge County bus had stopped to deposit a lone passenger on the side of the road. The driver helped the man off with his luggage, and something about his posture and movements looked vaguely familiar. He reminded me of someone, and I searched my mind hard to find a match.

The bus drove off in a cloud of dust and fumes, and the stranger looked up and down the road, obviously trying to get his bearings. He started to walk, hesitantly, in our direction. He looked my way, set his luggage down, and waved enthusiastically.

"Dad!" I shouted. "Dad!"

I covered the distance between us as fast as I could. I stopped hard a couple of feet in front of him and shook his hand warmly. Then, without even thinking about it, I leaned forward and hugged him. I felt some resistance, but he fought through the reflex and hugged back, properly, as if he really meant it.

"Henry," he said, "I am so very sorry about your friend Graham."

"Thanks, Dad."

He looked me squarely in the eye. "I wanted to come because I knew how badly you would feel. I didn't want you to have to go through something like this on your own."

I picked up his suitcase and we started toward the cottage. We walked silently for a few moments. And, as we did, I realized that what he had said was true. To go through a difficult experience without your family is to go through it essentially alone. Lily, and Charlie, and Jennifer were all wonderful. Ned and Mary had been supportive too. My experience in the church, realizing the part faith had to play, certainly made an impact. Running into old Mr. Kemp earlier in the day had helped recalibrate my attitude. But there was no substitution for my own family – there never is. Still, I felt amazed that my dad understood it all that well.

"I've taken Monday off so we can make a long weekend of it," he said. "I wanted to have a good chance to talk with you, get a feel for how you are living up here, and see what you do."

"That would be, err... great," I said, cautiously.

"I have come to suspect that one of the reasons we have been so at odds is that we don't really know each other anymore." Dad smiled, as if he were amused at the idea that a father and a son could possibly be strangers. But he was right. Practically speaking, we were.

"With your permission," he continued, in his inimitable style, "I would like to take steps to rectify the situation."

"That's really great," I said. "Absolutely. I am one hundred percent in agreement with you."

Then we were at the door. Lily made all sorts of noise and excitement, and my dad apologized for the inconvenience of such an impromptu visit. I, of course, offered to sleep on the floor for a couple of days and Lily – in characteristic fashion – conjured up an elaborate and improbable (in light of the rationing situation) table full of afternoon tea.

Later in the evening, after darkness has settled in, my dad announced that he was tired, and would like to make an early night of it.

"I've been travelling for several hours, and I'd like to be refreshed enough to enjoy the day around Isleham with Henry tomorrow."

"Dad," I said. "We heard that Mr. Jones got a catch in from his brother on the coast. Jennifer and I were talking about going out for some fish and chips this evening. Would you like to join us?"

"Thank you, but no. You young people eat a little extra on my behalf. But here," he said, handing me a shilling, "the treat is on me. Good night, all."

"Good night, Dad. I'm glad you're here."

Jennifer and I started out toward the village center. The fish and chip shop still stayed open late on Saturdays, even though the war had put a damper on business and sometimes all Mr. Jones had was just chips.

"Your dad's adorable!" she said. "Are you sure this is the same man you were talking about when you first came here?"

I laughed. "I think 'adorable' might be pushing it a little far. But I understand what you're saying. I have a question in answer to yours, though."

"Shoot," she said.

"Am I the same person as the Henry Bradley who first started telling you about his dad, back in the beginning of the summer?"

She looked at me thoughtfully.

"No," Jennifer said, squeezing my hand and then not letting go, "you most certainly are not."

CHAPTER TWENTY-SEVEN

A Huge Step in the Right Direction

Spending the day around Isleham with my father turned out to be more interesting than I could have hoped for.

I did manage to start in good style by serving him the classic "cup of tea in bed" before he got up in the morning. Then we enjoyed an early breakfast, where Lily let me cook up my version of the "farmhouse breakfast". After that, I took him out for an extended walking tour of the village, including much of the farm. We were accompanied, of course, by Newton, who was on his very best behavior.

At eleven o'clock we slipped into the small church, joining Lily, Jennifer, Charlie, and the others. There were more people in the pews than I remembered seeing before. It was as if the war had jogged people out of the casual disinterest that typically directed their Sunday mornings.

Jennifer held my hand during the sermon, and the minister actually had some interesting things to say. I don't know, maybe "the incident with the bee" had given him something to think about. Or maybe it was me, maybe I had been nudged out of my indifference, my tendency to take things lightly, my habit of not listening?

My dad was trying extra hard, I could tell, and together we were making a creditable effort. But it was difficult for him. We really hadn't spent much time together in a long while, even home in Folkestone, and we hadn't been tolerant of one another for even longer. I knew it would be all too easy – for both of us – to slip back into the destructive roles we had grown accustomed to.

Cynicism, criticism, obstinacy, lack of cooperation - these traits were such a pattern for our relationship that, even with all the good will and intention in the world, it would take some serious practice and attention to reverse the cumulative damage.

But we did both want to do better. I did love my dad – and he loved me – that much was obvious. And it was this positive ambition that made the day so enjoyable.

"I was really proud of you this morning, Henry," my dad offered, as we strode down a country lane to look at some of the bales of hay Charlie and I had helped Ned complete just a few days previously.

"Thanks, Dad. Why?"

"The sense of responsibility, care, and initiative you have demonstrated. Baling hay, getting up first in the morning, serving tea, making breakfast for the family - and doing it all so well. I had no idea you knew how to cook!"

"Neither did I," I said, not meaning to be funny, just honest. "But it turns out I enjoy it. Having Lily and Jennifer believe that I can contribute makes me feel good. Kind of like they trust me."

"Yes.... I see."

I let my dad feel the weight of a bale, and I told him about learning how to drive the tractor. He laughed out loud when I explained the missteps around my initial attempts, and he was obviously pleased with all I was learning. He told me he had wanted to spend a summer on a farm since he was a small boy, but always ended up working in his father's office, filing documents and adding up interminable lines of figures.

"Grandfather William wanted me to be an accountant," he said, sighing with a kind of wistful sadness.

"So why didn't you study agriculture when you went to the university?" I asked.

"Well," he said, "sometimes there's a difference between a father's pride and the dreams of his son. Your grandfather was, well, somewhat overbearing at times..."

My father hesitated, as if unable to go on.

"Kind of like you pushing me to be a doctor," I ventured cautiously, hoping I wasn't about to spoil a good thing by being maybe a little too honest, a little too soon.

He looked at me for a moment, considering his response, weighing his tone before launching.

"To be honest, Henry," he said, searching carefully for the right words, "not exactly. You see, at this point I am not aware of any subject or course of study you are even vaguely excited about in school. If there's anything that captures your imagination in that way, then I'm sure I don't know about it yet."

Well, I had to admit that he had me there.

"As regards your career choice, Henry, I'd be happy to see you engage me in debate to advance an alternate point of view, if you really do have the passion. However, in the absence of some kind of enthusiastic 'Plan B' coming from you, then medicine is not an unreasonable choice."

"Dad," I said, clearing my throat and taking a deep breath. "Showing up like you did yesterday, without Mum, it was a real surprise, really great."

I looked at him cautiously, wondering quite how far to go, how candid I should be. "It's something I would have expected Mum to do. But you, by yourself? Not in a million years."

"Really Henry? Does me being here for the weekend feel so dramatically out of character?" He looked genuinely puzzled; maybe a little hurt, but not angry or offended.

"Not so much out of character," I proceeded gingerly, "so much as out of practice - more like different from what I would have expected after these last couple of years. I don't think I've let myself see you as a potential friend in a long time, far too long. It may be that I just haven't understood you clearly, and that I haven't been paying enough attention to who you really are - because I'm always reacting when I should be listening."

I thought about Jennifer's advice to speak from my heart, to just be honest. I hoped she would be proud of me. I continued.

"Once I felt that I didn't know you anymore, then maybe it became more and more difficult for you too, impossible for us to connect. Kind of a mess that just kept on getting messier."

My father looked at me without flinching. "I think I understand exactly what it is that you're saying."

We spent a good hour looking around the old parish church. He had always been fond of architecture, and was quite excited by the craftsmanship and the classic Romanesque work we saw there.

Then we walked down to the village green. A makeshift cricket game was under way, and for the first time he told me something about his sad career as a cricket player in school.

"I wanted so much to be good at it," he laughed. "But I made a complete fool of myself several times."

I could see the disappointment still lingering in his eyes. So I told him about our recent game at Charter Academy. I could tell the story made him both proud and wistful all at the same time.

We sat on the bench and talked about my mother, about how badly it hurt her when there was conflict in our home. "Your mum would have come too if we could have made it work, Henry," he said. "But I'm glad it was me. I felt this was an important opportunity to make amends."

"I'm glad it was you, too," I said, earnestly. "It's not really anyone's fault, Dad. We just lost touch. I'm sorry, I truly am. I don't want to let it happen again."

"Nor me, Henry," he said. "Nor me."

CHAPTER TWENTY-EIGHT

A Magical Moment of Pain and Joy

Bright and early Monday morning, Lily, Jennifer, and I drove my dad back into Newmarket to catch the train. I had thought for a while that I would be going back to Folkestone with him. It was what I initially wanted, and what I had hoped for ever since we had arrived in Cambridgeshire back in early June. But the more I reasoned with myself about all the implications, the less sense it made.

First off, the tragic death of my friend Graham actually reinforced my dad's original, "I don't want to be the one responsible for leaving my son in harm's way if one of those bombs comes in through our living room window," argument. It was the idea that had been so hard for me to accept in the first place, and now it owned added credibility via his authentic caring. I had no comeback, and no desire to argue.

Second - and I believe that this was also related to Graham's death – was the fact that I could not in good conscience leave Charlie out there in the middle of nowhere all by himself. Besides,

I couldn't imagine Folkestone without the other two of *The Three Musketeers* (although Charlie and I were both going to have to accept the reality of Graham's absence when we did eventually get back home).

My experience with war was short, I understood that, but I already knew there was never any way to go back, that there is never any way to recreate the past. Besides, if I was completely honest I would have to admit that the past wasn't all that ideal either. I knew I didn't want to go backwards when it came to my dad. And I understood there was no way that returning to Folkestone would ever bring back my friend.

More importantly, and part of that difficult truth, I was most definitely not the same person who had first arrived, clutching my small suitcase of possessions, at the beginning of the summer. I was older, and it wasn't simply a matter of the sixteenth birthday. I knew so much more.

The shift in me was everything. It was Winston Churchill's speech, the hours of work in the fields, falling for Jennifer, and learning from Abraham - who had been through hell at the hands of the Nazis. It was the horrible fact of Graham's death. It was the surprising letter, and then the surprising visit, from home. It was listening to Mr. Kemp's story from the trenches of The Great War. It was the reconciliation that I knew in my heart was already underway with my dad.

I had no doubt – staying right there in Isleham was exactly the correct decision for me. There was much that I was learning, and still such a great deal for me one day to understand. Lily was marvelous, the farm was exhilarating, and my dad's short visit reminded me that my parents were not completely inaccessible.

And then there was Jennifer.

Jennifer. For the first time in my life I was being seriously bothered by a girl. Everything about her was becoming more and more intriguing. I wanted to know her more. I wanted to meet Mr. Spitfire and Mrs. Hush-Hush. I wanted to talk about books, and feelings, and ideas, and Graham, and the war. I wanted to hold her hand. I wanted to kiss her again, under another tree.

We all spilled out at the train station. Jennifer and Lily said goodbye, and then my dad and I walked up the slope to the platform, where his train was just pulling in. Steam billowed from the locomotive, a sharp hiss over the noise of doors opening and the rumble of luggage carts trundling.

Behind us, a woman with a small child hung desperately from the neck of a young man in uniform, crying. Two brisk businessmen in bowler hats walked deliberately onto the platform and then into a carriage, looking straight ahead and purposeful. Toward the end of the train a guard started closing doors, with a rhythmical clunk-pause-clunk-pause-clunk, alerting us to the imminent departure of the only morning train to London.

"Goodbye, Henry."

"Goodbye, Dad. Tell Mum I love her."

He extended his hand, gripping mine tightly. Silence hung in the air - heavy, dense, compressed in the moment. It was more solid than the clunking doors, louder than the hissing steam.

"I love you, Dad," I said. He met my gaze, started to say something in return, and stopped himself before pulling me firmly to him for a bear hug. Then, suddenly, he let go and mounted the steps quickly, shutting the door tight. It was the last car at the end of the train. He peered through the dirty window to where I stood, tears half filling my eyes.

The locomotive let out an extra-long hiss of steam, the engineer pulled the shrill whistle and slowly, almost imperceptibly at first, the hulking train began to move. I walked alongside, gradually quickening my step to keep up with my dad's position, wondering to myself if anything had really changed at all.

It was then, as the train's momentum began to build, that I saw my dad's hands go up. He pulled down the dirty window, and I could see him clearly, leaning out slightly and just ahead as I started to trot. He cupped his hands around his mouth.

"Henry," he yelled, urgently. "I love you. I – love – you - Henry!"

It was my father, Dr. Dignified himself, with his head hanging out of the window, a genuine smile on his face, and his rigid formality nowhere to be seen. He waved at me enthusiastically, honestly, without a care as to who might have been looking.

I may have been saved in that moment, as I look back and think about it from the space and distance of time. Knowing now what I didn't know then, understanding the timeless ramifications had he not said those words – yelled those words – in my direction. In fact I am sure of it. Those three words most likely saved the rest of my life.

*   *   *   *

I smiled broadly, and I waved frantically in my dad's direction. Then I stopped running – I didn't need to anymore, and I watched the train finally gather enough speed to leave me behind, exit the platform, round the long curve, and head out toward Cambridge, London, and eventually Folkestone – closer to the teeth of the war.

I stood there, breathless, at the far end of the platform, suspended in a magical moment of pain and joy. Behind me the train station emptied, while to the East the morning sun continued to rise, its warming rays promising the most glorious of summer days. I remained motionless, panting, watching the diminishing speck of the London train until, finally, I blinked my eyes and it was gone.

And when I turned around, walking slowly back to the exit, I thought about how hopeful the world could be. Even in the midst of shattering conflict, huge forces unleashing their vast machines of war, people could move closer to each other, families could learn to love again, and we could – all - finally begin to heal.

The entire continent of Europe was at war: bombs, missiles, armies, hate hurled from nation to nation, the lives of millions of people utterly destroyed. The threat of death and destruction was now of a magnitude never before imagined in the history of the planet. Yet, the simple human emotion of love could be more powerful, the possibility of reconciliation more compelling, the dawning of any new day – this one – still mine.

I started to climb into Lily's old truck. But then I stopped, looking back once more to the thin ribbon of rail disappearing into the horizon. Out of the corner of my eye I caught the glimpse of a trail of smoke to the southeast. It looked like a damaged German bomber limping away from some errant raid, unable to make headway toward the continent of Europe and home. The pilot was obviously fighting hard to stay in the air.

I hope he makes it, I thought. *I don't want anyone else in the world to lose a friend – especially someone they may not have realized quite how much they love.*

- finis -

Derek Maul

A NOTE ON THE HISTORICAL CONTEX

- 2017

This novel, as noted previously, is conceived as a work of historical fiction. I have, to the best of my ability, placed the characters in the context of an accurate retelling of life in England, at war, in the year 1940.

All the characters, including the protagonist, are entirely made up. But Henry and his friends lived is the very real town of Folkestone, the home where I grew up, very happily, from 1956 through 1974.

In 1940, Folkestone schools were evacuated immediately after Dunkirk (including children who had been sent to Folkestone from London in the fall of 1939) – this historical fact is consistent with Henry's account. As to location, Folkestone schools were sent to Wales. I chose Newmarket because of the beautiful setting and my familiarity with the area, having worked on an Isleham farm as a teen.

Winston Churchill's famous comments – "We shall fight on the beaches... we shall never surrender..." – are taken from a transcript of his radio broadcast shortly after Dunkirk.

I learned a lot about the evacuation experience from my parents, Grace and David Maul. My father was evacuated from Rayleigh, Essex when he was twelve years old, along with his school. He stayed in the town of Mansfield almost four years. The "pick a child" scenario I described is disturbingly accurate. My mother was sent away from East London when she was eight, but soon returned home for the duration of the war. Not a single one of the characters, or their families, in any way resembles my parents, aunts, uncles, or grandparents.

War is a terrible thing, always. But the accounts of regular people, caught up in extraordinary times, remain some of the most inspirational stories we know.

I hope you enjoyed the book (if you did, please review it on Amazon and recommend "Suddenly the Light was Gone" to your friends). I pray that we all remain committed to work for peace. It's never too late to learn from the stories – if only we are willing to listen.

Peace, in every way – Derek Maul

Made in the USA
Lexington, KY
02 October 2017